Kristy's Big News

Other books by
Ann M. Martin

P.S. Longer Letter Later
(written with Paula Danziger)
Leo the Magnificat
Rachel Parker, Kindergarten Show-off
Eleven Kids, One Summer
Ma and Pa Dracula
Yours Turly, Shirley
Ten Kids, No Pets
Slam Book
Just a Summer Romance
Missing Since Monday
With You and Without You
Me and Katie (the Pest)
Stage Fright
Inside Out
Bummer Summer

THE KIDS IN MS. COLMAN'S CLASS series
BABY-SITTERS LITTLE SISTER series
THE BABY-SITTERS CLUB mysteries
THE BABY-SITTERS CLUB series
CALIFORNIA DIARIES series

Baby-sitters Club

Friends BSC Forever

Kristy's Big News

Ann M. Martin

AN
APPLE
PAPERBACK

SCHOLASTIC INC.
New York   Toronto   London   Auckland   Sydney
Mexico City   New Delhi   Hong Kong

The author gratefully acknowledges
Nola Thacker
for her help in
preparing this manuscript.

Special thanks to Robin Dorman.

ISBN 0-590-52313-9

12 11 10 9 8 7 6 5 4 3 2 1   9/9 0 1 2 3 4/0

Printed in the U.S.A.   40

First Scholastic printing, August 1999

❊ Chapter 1

My stepfather, Watson Brewer, a mild-mannered millionaire, raised his fork and tapped his water glass. Normally, my family would probably not even notice the sound of a fork against a glass. Our family is large and very vocal, and tonight we were all talking even more than usual. It was the first dinner with every single one of us present since practically the beginning of the summer.

But this was Watson, and for him, tapping a fork on the side of his water glass at dinner is the same as one of us (me, maybe) shouting "QUIET" at the top of her lungs.

Everyone became quiet.

Watson smiled at all of us and raised his glass. "Here's to the approach of a new school year" (my older brother Charlie groaned loudly, but we ignored him) "and to our being together for this end-of-the-summer dinner."

We raised our glasses, and my mother added, "To us."

I took a ceremonial sip of water and put my glass down. The roar of talk resumed almost immediately, but I didn't join in. I looked around at the other nine people at the table. We were, I had to admit, a most excellent family.

But we haven't always been such a *big* family. Not long ago, there were only five of us: my mother, Elizabeth; my older brothers, Charlie and Sam (now seventeen and fifteen); my younger brother, David Michael (now seven); and me, Kristy Thomas (I'm thirteen).

My father, Patrick, walked out on us when David Michael was a baby. He ended up in California. Back here in Stoneybrook, Connecticut, we rarely heard from him. Nor did we have much time to think about him. We were too busy struggling to make ends meet.

It wasn't easy, but it wasn't terrible either. Because, as corny as it sounds, we knew we could count on one another. And then Mom met Watson Brewer. They fell in love and got married, and we moved across town — from the house we'd always lived in on Bradford Court, to Watson's mansion, where he lived with his daughter, Karen (now age seven); and his son, Andrew (now age four). They live here every other month and spend the alternate months with their mom, who has also remarried and lives nearby.

I'm not kidding about the mansion. It's a real mansion, with room enough for every one of us, plus assorted pets and even what Karen, who has a very vivid imagination, claims is the ghost of one of her ancestors, Ben Brewer.

Not long after the move, we adopted Emily Michelle (now two and a half), who was born in Vietnam. Then my maternal grandmother, whom we call Nannie, came to live with us also, to help with Emily Michelle and to restore order to creeping chaos.

I wasn't sure at first how I was going to like these changes. After all, we'd been managing pretty well. And given the way my father had disappeared on us, I wasn't sure I liked the idea of another father or stepfather.

Then again, Watson was very different from Patrick — or at least from what I could remember about him. My father was forever moving, restless, picking something up and putting it down as he talked, walking back and forth with his hands stuck in his pockets, playing tennis with ferocious intensity, or totally immersing himself in whatever interested him at the moment. Sometimes I think that his restlessness was one of the reasons he left us: He picked us up and then put us down and walked on to something new.

Watson, on the other hand, is a thoughtful and serious man. He is the CEO of Unity Insurance, and he works hard — so hard that he even had a mild heart attack not long ago. But he's obeying the doctor's orders to ease up a little, and he seems in good health again.

Watson's ruling passion, after family and maybe before work, is one he shares with Nannie: gardening. You'd be more likely to find him arguing with her over the advice in a gardening magazine, or digging a hole for a new Japanese maple tree, one of his favorites, than charging around a tennis court (although you might find him covering first in a baseball game — he *loves* baseball and plays a tough game).

Watson is quiet and deliberate. He's also patient and kind, and I soon realized I couldn't have asked for a better stepfather. I love him very much now.

Watson's head was bent as he listened to something that Karen, her blue eyes round behind her glasses, was telling him. My mother was smiling fondly at them both. I heard Nannie say, "Good, Emily Michelle," and watched as my youngest sister spooned up some mashed potatoes without dropping any on herself or on the table. On the other side of her, Andrew was piling his peas into a nest he'd built of the mashed potatoes. Charlie had shown him how to make a mashed-potato nest with green-pea eggs, and now it was one of Andrew's favorite dishes. My grin widened as I realized that Charlie was doing the exact same thing. Sam and David Michael were talking about baseball. Listening in, I realized that they had the completely wrong idea about who was going to win the World Series in October.

I was about to jump in with my opinion when the phone rang. My mother automatically stood up to answer it.

"Let the answering machine pick it up," suggested Watson, but my mom had already slipped through the door into the kitchen. It's funny, but she always thinks that if someone calls late at night or during dinner, it must be an emergency. After all, who would be rude enough to interrupt people otherwise?

Telemarketers, I thought. Idly, I wondered who

was calling our house, trying to sell what, and how long it would take my mom to persuade them never to call again. In the meantime, I decided to set Sam and David Michael straight about the Series. By the time Mom returned, I was so involved in a debate over who had a deeper pitching staff that I didn't even notice Mom's expression — at least not until Nannie said, "Elizabeth? What's wrong?"

We all looked up, and I saw Watson's eyebrows draw together slightly. Mom's warm brown eyes appeared puzzled and the rest of her normally animated face was almost blank. She was standing by her chair, resting her hands on top of it.

"Mom?" I said.

Mom reached out and touched Watson's hand as he reached for hers, and then smiled. I was reassured. It couldn't be too serious.

"Don't worry," she said. "Everything's fine."

"Who called?" asked Watson.

"Patrick," she said. "It's Patrick."

For a moment, I wasn't sure who she was talking about. Then I thought, *It's my father.*

Mom looked from me to Charlie, to Sam, to David Michael. "He's still on the phone," she said. "He wants to talk to you, Kristy, and to Charlie and Sam. He has some . . . some important news for you."

❀ Chapter 2

"What is it?" I blurted out. I pushed my chair back and stood up. I couldn't think. My father never, *ever* calls us. Never. In fact, I've only seen him a handful of times since he left, including once completely by chance at a ball game in California.

"Kristy?" my mother said in a gentle voice.

"Go on," Watson said. "Why don't you use the extension in my office?"

I nodded. I turned toward Watson's office, glad to have a little time to collect myself.

I hesitated a long moment before picking up the phone. This was a clear sign that I was rattled. Any of my friends will tell you that I do *not* hesitate often.

I picked up the phone, pressed it to my ear, and said, "Hello?"

"Kristy!" My father's voice boomed over the line as if we were old buddies. "Is that you?"

"Yes," I said. "Uh, hi. How are you?"

"Oh, fine, fine. Better than fine. Excellent, in fact." My father sounded nervous — and way too cheerful. What was going on?

Charlie said from another phone, "Why are you calling?"

"Well, because I have great news. Everyone's on now, right? Sam, Charlie?" Without waiting for an answer, my father continued, "I wanted my kids to be the first to know: I'm getting married. To Zoey. That's her name. She's great."

No one said a word. It was as if the phone connection between California and Stoneybrook had been cut off.

My father said, "Aren't you going to congratulate me?"

I heard a click. Somehow, I knew it was Charlie, hanging up the phone.

Patrick didn't seem to notice. "Well?" he said. "Don't all rush in at once."

Sam said, "Congratulations."

"Congratulations," I mumbled.

"And that's not all," Patrick said, the pitch of his voice increasing and making him sound even more nervous. Maybe he had noticed a slight lack of enthusiasm at our end, I thought. "I want you all to come to my — our — wedding."

"School's about to start," Sam began. "I don't think — "

"It's next Saturday," Patrick interrupted. "Your mother says it's up to you guys, and I know you want to be here. Your plane tickets are already on the way by Fed Ex. They'll be there tomorrow."

"But — " Sam tried again.

"Everything's taken care of," Patrick said. "Will you come? Sam?"

"I guess," answered Sam. "If it's okay with Mom."

"Kristy?"

I wanted to say no, but I couldn't. "Okay."

"Charlie?"

"He had to get off the phone," I said. It was the truth. "But he'll let you know."

"Oh. Well. He'll be there. I know my kids won't let me down. This is terrific!"

Not quite, I couldn't help thinking.

"Put your mother back on, would you?"

"I'll get her," I said quickly. " 'Bye." I couldn't say the word "Dad." Somehow, it just didn't fit my father anymore. I set the phone down and returned to the dining room. Sam was sliding into his chair as if his knees weren't working right. Charlie's face was stony. "He wants to talk to you again," I said to my mom.

I followed Mom down the hall and into the study. She picked up the phone and she didn't hesitate. "Well?" she said. Her voice was calm and expressionless. She listened for a moment and said, "We're in the middle of dinner. I'd prefer to discuss this later."

She listened again, looked up, and said, "Wait a minute." She put her hand over the mouthpiece and said to me, "Kristy, go on. Finish your dinner."

Whatever my mother had to say to Patrick, she wanted to say it in private.

Reluctantly, I left the study and rejoined the rest of my family.

Nannie was shaking her head. She hadn't even noticed that Emily Michelle had reverted to eating her mashed potatoes with her fingers. Watson was sitting very still, and David Michael and Andrew looked like smaller versions of him. Karen was bouncing up and down.

Sam had told them, I knew. The tension in the room was almost visible.

"Kristy," Watson said with a smile. I was relieved

to see it was his normal Watson smile. I managed to smile back.

"Well, it won't be a June wedding," said Watson, "but out in California the weather should be wonderful."

No one said anything. Watson turned to Nannie. "Excellent gardening country out there. Farther up the coast, in Oregon and Washington, they grow some of the best apples in the world."

Nannie said, almost automatically, "Don't forget New York apples."

Charlie said, "I'm not going."

Then David Michael asked, "Can I go?" and the conversation stopped again. It was only then that I realized that my father had not asked his youngest son to come to the phone, had not told him the news, and had not invited him to the wedding.

Had he forgotten David Michael? Surely not. Maybe he just thought David Michael was too young for the trip.

Charlie fixed burning eyes on Sam and said, as if David Michael hadn't spoken, "Are you?"

Sam nodded. "I said I would, I guess," he answered in a low voice.

Turning to me, Charlie asked, "And you?"

"I said I would."

"I want to go too," David Michael chimed in.

"Well, there's no way I'm going," Charlie announced.

As David Michael was about to speak again, I said, "Wait until Mom gets off the phone and talk to her."

Charlie said, "I can't believe you guys agreed to go to *his* wedding. Just like that."

"He's my real father. I want to go," insisted David Michael.

Did I see Watson flinch? I hoped not. I hoped his feelings weren't hurt. David Michael had spoken without thinking, but he was only seven.

"Your real father," Charlie sputtered. "A real father doesn't go off and leave his family. I was ten when he left. I remember what it was like. I remember how Mom — "

He stopped abruptly as Mom returned. She pulled her chair out from the table and sat down. She made an elaborate show of putting her napkin on her lap. Only then did she look around. A spot of color glowed on each cheek. She took a deep breath. "We have a lot to talk about," she said.

If I hadn't been so upset I might have laughed. It wasn't the understatement of the year — it was the understatement of my whole life.

Chapter 3

The tickets arrived early the next morning.

David Michael, Karen, and Andrew were in the backyard, playing with Shannon, our Bernese mountain dog puppy. Watson and Nannie were in full gardening gear: gloves, hats, old jeans, workshirts. (Watson sometimes works at home now, which means he can make his own hours.) I watched them through the kitchen window as I finished my solitary breakfast of cereal (Wheaties mixed with Rice Krispies). They were staring up into the branches of a holly tree on one side of the house. It was hard to tell whether they were going to prune it or try to make it levitate.

I put my dishes in the dishwasher and carried my o.j. into the family room, where Mom was dressed for work, watching Emily Michelle empty the contents of an old purse onto the rug and put everything back into it again. This included an old key ring, a small stuffed animal, a soft alphabet block, and various other items. Mom was holding a cup of coffee and talking to Emily Michelle. "Blue," I heard her say as I came into the room. "That piece of velvet is blue. Can you say blue?"

Emily Michelle put the piece of velvet up to her cheek for a moment, then put it in the purse and pounced on the old key ring.

"Hi, Mom," I said.

"Kristy," she said. "Good morning."

"I guess," I said. I felt heavy-eyed and stupid. Normally, I'm the first one up, but the night before I'd stared into the dark a long time before falling asleep. Now I was sluggish, and my breakfast was sitting in a lump in my stomach.

Mom smiled a little as if she understood. She looked a little sleepy herself. "I think it's going to be another perfect day," she said.

"I guess," I said again. "I wonder what the weather is like in California."

A short pause followed. Then Mom said, "Kristy, I don't know what to say about all this. I'm still . . . I can't . . . I just don't know."

This was not reassuring. I think I'd sort of been counting on Mom to have it all figured out.

"Oh," I said.

That's when the doorbell rang.

"I'll get it," I said. I don't know who I expected it to be — maybe one of my friends who'd somehow sensed I needed her.

But it wasn't. It was a Fed Ex delivery person. When I saw her I said, "Oh, it's you."

She didn't seem to notice the odd greeting. I signed for the package and walked back to the family room, eyeing the label. Was that my father's handwriting? I couldn't be sure. I had studied the collection of cards (numbering in the single digits) he'd sent me over the years until I knew them all by heart, but still, I couldn't be sure.

Silently, I handed the package to Mom.

She took it and opened it, pulling out three airline tickets to California: one for me, one for Sam, one for Charlie.

None for David Michael.

A voice said from the doorway, "I'm not going."

Charlie was standing there, scowling. We all looked up at him, even Emily Michelle. Then she went back to reloading the handbag.

"Charlie," Mom began.

"No," said Charlie. "Why should I? After what he did to us?"

I stared at Charlie. He'd never talked much about what had happened, even though he was the one of us kids who probably remembered our father best. For awhile, I'd been jealous that he had those memories and I didn't. But lately I'd begun to see the advantages of not being able to remember much about a father who was there one day and gone the next.

I'd cried at first, all those years ago, late at night when I thought no one could hear me. Had Charlie cried? Or had he tried not to, because he shared a room with Sam?

Charlie's face was set and hard. He looked a lot older than seventeen.

Mom took a deep breath. "It's up to you, Charlie," she said. "But I hope you'll reconsider."

"I won't," he said. He turned and left abruptly.

"He'll change his mind," I said, more confidently than I felt. "There's time." I paused, then added, "Isn't there? I mean, when do we leave?"

"Monday," said Mom. "You fly out Monday. The wedding's the following Saturday, and the return tickets are for Sunday."

"That's practically a whole week!" I exclaimed. "Where are we going to stay?"

A funny look crossed Mom's face. "With your father."

That stopped me. I hadn't spent a whole week with my dad since I was about six. Something like panic flooded me — panic, and anger. Suddenly my father was getting married, and just like that I was supposed to go spend a whole week with him? Why hadn't he wanted me around before?

But I couldn't say that to Mom. I bit my lip and then said, "I'm going to go over to Mary Anne's, okay?"

"Sure," said Mom. She picked up Emily Michelle and pressed her chin to the top of Emily's head.

I bolted for the door almost as abruptly as Charlie had.

Mary Anne Spier and I have known each other since we were both babies. We used to live next door to each other on Bradford Court, before Mom married Watson and we moved. Mary Anne's father got remarried to Sharon, his high school sweetheart, not long after that, and they moved too, to a house on the edge of town. (Sharon's daughter, Dawn, is Mary Anne's other best friend as well as her stepsister. She lives in California now with her brother, her father, and his new wife). In fact, Mary Anne and I were at that wedding, but that's another story. (Mary Anne's birth mother died when Mary Anne was just a baby, too little to remember her.)

But Mary Anne's back on Bradford Court now — for an awful reason. Her house was destroyed. Faulty electrical wiring caused it to burn to the ground, with everything Mary Anne and her family owned inside. Luckily no one was hurt, not even Tigger, her gray tiger-striped kitten.

Anyway, Mary Anne now lives in a rental house across the street from her old house and next door to Claudia Kishi, another friend of ours.

Remembering what Mary Anne had been through helped me put things in perspective a little as I biked furiously across town to her house. I hoped she was home. I hadn't even bothered to call first.

She was — and she took one look at my face and said, "Kristy! What's wrong?"

That's Mary Anne for you. She not only knows me *way* too well, but she's very sensitive. She picks up on things that most other people would miss.

"My father," I said.

"Watson?"

"No! Not Watson. Patrick."

"Let's go to my room," said Mary Anne. "You can hold Tigger while you tell me about it. It's *very* soothing to hold a cat."

I had to laugh at her solution. But I followed her obediently through the still-unfamiliar halls of her new house.

As we sat down on the bed in her room, it creaked. Mary Anne made a face. "Rental furniture," she said. "When we get settled in a home of our own again, we're going to have new furniture."

"That'll be fun to shop for," I said.

"True. But . . ." Her voice trailed off. I knew what she was thinking. She would prefer not to be shopping for furniture at all. Losing everything in a fire was no way to go about getting a new wardrobe or practically a new life.

She scooped up Tigger from the pillow and plopped him on my lap. He settled in and turned his purr up a notch as I absently stroked his back.

"Patrick," Mary Anne prompted me.

"Okay. Well. It's like this. Patrick called last night, in the middle of dinner." I gave her the whole story, and she listened intently, her gaze never leaving my face.

"And Charlie absolutely refuses to go," I said. "I'm not sure I want to go either, but if Charlie doesn't go it's going to make things even weirder. And what about the extra ticket?"

"It's a problem," Mary Anne agreed.

At that point, I came up with one of my brilliant ideas. (I haven't mentioned, have I, that I'm famous for my brilliant ideas — such as thinking up the Baby-sitters Club? I have mentioned the BSC, haven't I? We meet regularly, although not as often as we used to, and clients know that with one phone call they can reach several experienced, reliable baby-sitters. We're so well known now in Stoneybrook that we don't even have to advertise.) "Wait a minute," I cried. "I've got it!"

"What?"

"The answer. The solution. You!" I pointed at Mary Anne.

"Me? Me what?"

"You can go to the wedding too. In Charlie's place. Or even if he does decide to go."

"Kristy . . ."

"It makes perfect sense, Mary Anne. Think about it. It would make everything *much* easier if you went with me."

"Kristy . . ." Mary Anne tried again. I rolled right over her.

"Plus, when Dawn's dad remarried, I went to

California with you for that, remember? So it's only fair that you go to California with me for Patrick's wedding. What a *great* idea. If I do say so myself."

"It would be nice to go to California," said Mary Anne diplomatically. "But I think this time it would be better if I didn't go. This is a family thing, Kristy, something you and your brothers should do on your own."

"Don't you want to go to California with me?" I asked.

"You know I'd love to."

"We could visit Dawn."

"California's a big state," Mary Anne replied. "Where does Patrick live?"

That stopped me. "He used to live in Sausalito," I said. "I'm not sure if he still does."

And, come to think of it, I wasn't even sure how far Sausalito was from where Dawn lived.

"Well, even if he lived next door to Dawn, I couldn't go with you, Kristy. You know that," Mary Anne said.

I sighed. "Yeah, I know. But I wish you could."

"I wish I could too." Mary Anne paused to let my not-so-brilliant idea die a natural death, then changed the subject, sort of. "Did Patrick tell you who he's marrying? What do you think she's like?"

*   *   *

Claudia came over later, and I ended up calling Watson and spending the rest of the day at Mary Anne's. At five-thirty we met up at Claudia's house with our friend Stacy McGill, for a BSC meeting. We made plans for every possible baby-sitting emergency while I was gone. After all, I am the president of the BSC. It's my job to make sure the club runs smoothly, even when I'm not there. I went home after the meeting feeling a little less confused and chaotic inside. But our house was still in a quiet uproar. As I walked into the kitchen to see if I could help with dinner, I heard David Michael say, "But I *want* to go. Charlie doesn't want to go, and I do. Why can't I?"

Karen and Andrew were setting the table. Karen was talking to Andrew about the secret life of dogs, explaining that dogs and cats and all animals talked all the time, when humans weren't listening. Andrew was watching Shannon out of the corner of his eye. Shannon, who didn't seem to have anything to say for herself at the moment, was lying on her pillow in a corner of the kitchen, chomping on a Nylabone.

"Hi," I said to Watson, who was standing at the stove, stirring something. "I'm home."

"Kristy," he said, looking pleased.

"What're we having for dinner?"

"Gnocchi," answered Watson.

"Potato lumps," said Karen, coming to watch Watson stir. "We helped boil the potatoes and then Daddy mashed them with eggs and now we're boiling them again."

"It's a sort of potato pasta, like little dumplings," Watson interjected.

"Sounds good. What can I do to help?"

"Call in the troops," said Watson, lifting a spoonful of the little dumplings onto a plate. "We're ready to eat."

Maybe things had settled down, I reasoned as I obeyed Watson. I managed to hold onto that hope even when I found Charlie in his room with the door closed. "Coming," he growled when I knocked and told him it was time for dinner.

I thought of trying to talk to Charlie, but what could I say? My oldest brother is a stand-up kind of guy, patient as the day is long. It takes a lot to make him lose it.

But now he was angry, and our father's invitation to the wedding was responsible. I didn't know how to talk to him about it.

Maybe time would cool him off, I thought. Maybe that was all we needed — a little time. Maybe the rest of the family was already adjusting to the news.

Wrong, and wrong again.

"Why can't *I* go to California?" were the first words I heard from David Michael as he followed Mom into the kitchen. She had just walked in the door and was still wearing her work clothes.

"There isn't a ticket for you," Mom said. "I think your father felt that you aren't quite old enough to — "

"There's a ticket if Charlie doesn't go," David Michael interrupted.

"I want to go to California too," Karen said out of the blue. "I like weddings. I don't have to be in it. I just want to go."

"Me too," Andrew said immediately. "I want to go too."

"There aren't any tickets for you either," my mother said.

Watson suggested, "Why don't we all sit down? These need to be eaten while they're still warm."

"Gnocchi," said Karen importantly, her attention diverted. "With mari . . . mari . . ."

"Marinara sauce," Watson said.

"Tomatoes," Karen explained.

"I'm not too young," said David Michael stubbornly.

"Let me serve you some gnocchi, David Michael," Watson said.

I could tell Mom was having a hard time satisfying David Michael's questions about why he hadn't been included. Was it true that Patrick had thought David Michael was too young? Why couldn't Patrick have told David Michael that himself?

Nannie concentrated on helping Emily Michelle. She held definite opinions about Patrick and always had. I'd overheard some of them over the years, when she'd been talking to Mom. But she'd never said anything to me, or to any of us kids that I knew of, and she didn't say anything now.

David Michael's voice slid into a whine. "It's not faaair. It's *not*. I want to go to California."

"You're not going," said Mom. The tone of her voice warned David Michael he was pushing his luck. He lowered his head, stuck out his lower lip, and poked at the food on his plate.

Poor guy, I thought. He was feeling left out, and his feelings were hurt. And poor Mom too.

Karen stopped talking about her need to go to the wedding and fell uncharacteristically silent.

Andrew began flattening his gnocchi with his fork, attempting to turn them back into mashed potatoes.

That left me, Sam, Watson, and Mom to make conversation. We tried. We tried very hard. But it was no use.

At the end of the meal, Charlie, who hadn't said a word, picked up his plate and stood up. "I just want to say that now I've thought it over, and I'm *still* not going to his wedding," he announced.

He turned to leave.

"Wait a minute," Mom said.

Charlie turned. I think he expected her to beg him to go or to try to reason with him. He looked angry and defiant.

But Mom surprised Charlie. She surprised us all, except maybe Watson. "Fine," she said to Charlie. "Don't go. But in that case, Kristy and Sam can't go either."

❀ Chapter 4

I couldn't believe it.

I sat down with Sam to watch a baseball game after dinner, but not even a perfect double play featuring a bare-handed catch and a behind-the-back toss by the shortstop to second could hold my attention for long. I kept thinking about what Charlie had said and what Mom had said then.

If Charlie didn't go to the wedding, neither Sam nor I could go either.

Suddenly, I realized how much I really wanted to see my father. I wasn't sure how I felt about his getting remarried, but maybe the wedding would be some kind of turning point. Maybe he'd be — what? More fatherlike? Or just, well, more there.

How did Sam feel? I wanted to ask him, but somehow I couldn't. He was sprawled in the overstuffed armchair, his arms folded, his eyes half closed. I knew he wasn't sleepy. I didn't think he was paying much attention to the game either.

Just to see, I picked up the remote and flicked to another channel.

"Hey," Sam mumbled. Normally, that move would have earned a howl of protest.

"Hey, yourself," I said. I surfed back to the baseball game. "You sorry to miss the wedding?"

Sam's eyelids lowered a fraction of an inch more. "Maybe. But at least this way I don't have to get all dressed up."

"*Sam.* I'm serious."

If Sam slid any lower in the chair, he was going to slide out of it.

"Sam?"

"Yeah, sure. I want to go. I think. I'd kind of like to see . . . him."

I set the remote on the table between us. "I'm going to talk to Charlie. Want to come?"

"Nah," said Sam. His eyes opened slightly and he glanced at me before glancing back at the screen. "But let me know how it goes."

"I will."

I knocked on Charlie's door and opened it before he even finished saying, "Who is it?"

"A member of your family," I said.

"I kind of thought it might be." He was propped on the bed, reading *The Sporting News*.

"I get to read that when you're finished," I said automatically.

Charlie said, "You came up here to tell me that?"

"No. Of course not." I sat down in the chair at his desk. "We need to talk."

"What about?" He held the paper up in front of him, like a line of scrimmage.

This annoyed me. Charlie is not dense. He knew what I wanted to talk about, and he was making it as hard as possible for me. I narrowed my eyes at him.

He lowered the paper then. "Kristy — " he began.

I didn't let him finish. "It's not fair, Charlie. What right do you have to . . . to . . . to sabotage the plans for the wedding?"

"He can have the wedding without me. Just like I can have a life without him."

I knew Charlie was angry at our father, but I had never heard him speak so bluntly or so bitterly. I took a deep breath, feeling hurt for Charlie and maybe for all of us. But I wasn't going to let that stop me. "You can have a life without Patrick," I agreed.

"We all can. But he's invited us to his wedding. It's important to him for us to be there."

"Then tell Mom how important it is," Charlie said, his own eyes as narrow as mine now.

"You know she won't change her mind. And you know, maybe she's right. If only two of us show up, what are we supposed to say? Sorry, Charlie is so angry at you that he's not coming?"

"That's his problem."

"Charlie!" Frustrated, I jumped to my feet and slapped both palms against the top of his desk. "Listen. This is important to me. It's important to Sam. And it's important to you, whether you'll admit it or not. If it wasn't important, you wouldn't be so angry. You just wouldn't care."

Charlie opened his mouth, shut it, glared at me.

"If you're afraid to see Patrick . . ." I went on.

"I'm not afraid. I just don't want to see him. I have nothing to say to him."

"Then go and don't say anything," I said. "But please, *please* don't keep us from going to the wedding. Because maybe I want to go and see if I *do* have something to say."

"This isn't fair," said Charlie.

"No, I guess it isn't," I agreed, to my own surprise.

I caught Charlie by surprise too. He stared at me, his face pale, with spots of color on his cheeks, the way he always looks when he's really intense about something, which isn't very often. I had a sense that Charlie could explode at any moment. I braced myself and waited.

Finally, he said, "I don't owe him anything."

"No," I said neutrally.

"If I went, it wouldn't be for him, it'd be for you and for Sam."

"Yes," I agreed, although I didn't think that was entirely true.

"Fine," said Charlie abruptly. "I'll go. I'll go, but I won't like it. If you're imagining some kind of cozy family reunion, count me out."

I let my breath out all at once. I hadn't realized I was holding it. "You will?" I said, just to make sure. "You'll go to the wedding with Sam and me?"

"I'll go," said Charlie, raising *The Sporting News* again.

"Thanks!" I said. I leaned over and punched him on the shoulder.

He made a face at me.

I turned to leave. "Hey," I said, stopping at the door.

He kept his eyes on the newspaper.

"Thanks."

"Yeah. Right," said my oldest brother.

I decided not to push my luck. I left, closing the door quietly behind me.

Sam hadn't moved. "Two out, bases loaded, top of the sixth," he said. "Our man at the plate is trying for a walk."

I sat down on the sofa and leaned back. I watched the batter begin to play a waiting game with the pitcher, scuffing his feet, stepping out of the box between each pitch.

I played a waiting game too.

The batter fouled the seventh pitch straight up and the catcher caught it for the third out.

Sam said, "Well?"

"He'll go," I said. "He doesn't like it, but he'll go."

"I don't like it so much either," my second-oldest brother said. He waited.

I waited.

Sam added, "But I'm glad. Thanks, Kristy."

"Yeah. Right," said his eldest younger sister.

❀ Chapter 5

I should know how to pack to go to a wedding, even one in California, right? I'm a veteran attendee of weddings: Mom and Watson's; Mary Anne's dad and Dawn's mom's; Dawn's dad's, in California.

But as I hurried to the car, dragging my suitcase, I was *sure* that I had forgotten something. Stopping on the sidewalk, I pulled the packing list out of my pocket and checked it once more.

I hadn't forgotten a thing.

From behind me Watson said, "Ready to put that in the van?" I nodded, worried for a moment that he shouldn't be lifting my suitcase because of his heart. Then I realized I was being a tad overprotective and forced myself not to protest. Sam was leaning against the van, looking bored.

"We're not late, are we?" I asked. "Where's Charlie?"

"We have plenty of time," Watson assured me. He smiled. "No backpack? No books for the plane?"

"My pack!" I yelped, and raced back into the house.

I returned with my pack as Charlie was swinging his suitcase into the rear of the van. Nannie, Emily Michelle, Karen, Andrew, and David Michael had come out on the porch to wave good-bye. David Michael's hand rested on Shannon's head. She was sitting by him, her tail swishing.

"When you get to California," said Karen, "don't get eaten by *sharks*."

Andrew frowned. I patted his shoulder. "Don't worry," I told him and Karen. "This wedding is strictly on dry land. No sharks." (I hoped that was true.)

Nannie kissed my cheek. "Be good," she said, just as she had said when I was little.

"I will," I promised.

"Have fun," said David Michael in a small voice. "Don't forget you said you'd send cool postcards."

I dropped down and put my arm around his shoulders. "I won't forget. And I'm going to call home, and then we'll all be back next week."

Mom had finally convinced David Michael that he was too young to go to the wedding, and that with me, Sam, and Charlie going, she needed him at home. He wasn't happy about it, but he'd accepted it at last. I'd talked to him too, a little, and promised him cool postcards and a surprise. That had helped, but I knew his feelings were hurt and nothing I could do would change that. And while I did think David Michael was too young to go to the wedding, I wished that it had been Patrick who'd worked it out with David Michael.

We waved good-bye and Watson drove us to the airport. After what seemed like an endless, awkward wait, we finally boarded the plane. We had three seats together. Charlie slid in next to the window, folded his arms, and stared out the window. I slid in next to him, and Sam sat on the aisle.

Sam leaned across me. "Thanks for asking," he said to Charlie.

"What?"

"About whether anyone else wanted to sit by the window."

"Oh," said Charlie. "Sorry. We can switch if you want."

"Why don't we take turns," I suggested. "After all, it's a long flight."

Charlie nodded and turned back to scrutinizing the wing of the plane.

I gave my list one more review and said, "The key. The house key? And the extra car keys?" (Neither Patrick nor Zoey could pick us up at the airport, so they'd left one of their cars in the lot, with the directions to the house in the glove compartment. Keys to the house and car had been in the overnight package.)

"In my pocket," said Charlie. "You saw Mom give them to me, Kristy. Stop worrying." He paused, then added, "Although maybe you should. I'd be surprised if Patrick remembered to leave the car. It'd be just like him to forget, the way he forgot about us all these years."

Before I could answer, the flight attendant began to recite the safety instructions. I decided to let it go. I settled back.

I stopped worrying about keys and luggage. I worried about Charlie. And Sam. And me. And what was going to happen at the wedding.

Charlie was plainly making the trip against his will. I felt awkward and guilty. But what could I do? Making him feel better about the situation seemed impossible. And besides, even I knew that there were some things I couldn't fix — such as how Charlie felt about our father.

Sam (who'd put on his headset and was listening to music) wasn't deep-down angry the way Charlie was. Or, at least, I didn't think so. He'd been enthusiastic about a free trip to California and carefully neutral about the wedding itself.

But now that I thought about it, Sam had always taken things less seriously than Charlie. He hid his emotions behind jokes and laughter.

How long had it been since I'd hung around with my two older brothers? I couldn't remember. When we were younger, when we'd been struggling to hold our family together after Patrick had left, we'd been together all the time. We'd all had chores and responsibilities, more than most kids.

Even though he'd been only ten, Charlie had been our main baby-sitter. He'd taken care of us after school, while Mom sat at the kitchen table doing bookkeeping for various small companies or studying to complete her degree in accounting. Sometimes she'd rock David Michael in her arms as she flipped pages.

But Charlie had taken care of David Michael most of the time, right down to diaper changing.

He'd kept us quiet while Mom worked, he'd kept us entertained, he'd kept us out of trouble — mostly.

I smiled suddenly, remembering the time Sam and I had "helped" by doing the laundry while Charlie was reading a story to David Michael. We'd gathered all our dirty clothes together, including a bright red shirt, and put them into the wash. Everything white had come out pink when the red shirt had run.

We'd been appalled, especially at the pink shirts we'd all have to wear. But Charlie had come up with a solution. We'd washed the formerly white clothes again, this time with a new bright yellow towel. The yellow dye on top of the pink had produced a sort of faded, weird orange — much easier to take than a school year in faded, weird pink.

If Mom had noticed, she'd never said a word.

She *had* noticed when Charlie gave us all haircuts to save money. He'd been so proud — we all had — and she had looked stunned. Somehow, she'd managed to keep her composure while telling us that we all looked so different she wouldn't have recognized us. She also managed to use the right words about taking us to the barber "just to get things evened up a little bit" so that our feelings wouldn't be hurt.

Our school pictures that year show us all with *extremely* short hair. Come to think of it, Sam is wearing a faded, weird orange shirt too.

Another memory returned suddenly: Charlie's face as he unwrapped a baseball glove on his eleventh birthday. It was from all of us, but I remember Sam had suggested it.

Charlie's face had glowed for a moment. Then he had said, "I can't."

"Yes you can," said Sam. "I'm almost ten. I can take care of things at least one day a week."

And Charlie, always careful to be fair, had said, "We can trade. One day a week."

Charlie hadn't played baseball the whole first year after our dad had left because he'd been needed at home after school. But only Sam had known how much that had meant to Charlie. Charlie, outwardly easygoing and untouched, had never said a word. And Sam, quiet and more observant than people realized, had known how much it meant to Charlie.

And they'd been careful to include me in their practice games of catch. That's one of the reasons I'm a softball coach now.

We'd been close back then. We'd taken care of one another. But then, somehow, as things became easier, we'd all gone in different directions. We weren't as close as we'd been.

Was that part of growing up? I wasn't sure I liked it.

Or maybe it was better that we were a family held together by love now, instead of an us-against-the-world family.

We didn't talk much the rest of the trip. Charlie brooded. Sam remained almost aloof, even when he took his turn at the window. I opted for the in-flight movie and then read until we started to descend. Then I elbowed Sam and made him switch places with me so I could watch us come down out of the clouds.

The car was just where Patrick had said it would be *and* the directions inside were neat, complete, and concise. Charlie raised his eyebrows in surprise, but he didn't say anything.

I was surprised too. I wasn't so surprised that the car and the directions were there, but I was surprised at the car: a sleek little blue Audi A4 with a sunroof. This didn't fit my image of Patrick the journalist, traveling the world with a suitcase and a battered typewriter (not a computer — typewriters could be used anywhere, even in a desert or a cave). I realized that a part of me had always believed that Patrick had left us to pursue his dream of being a journalist, the kind who could take off at the drop of a hat in search of a story.

It could still be true, I reassured myself. This must be Zoey's car. After all, the directions weren't in my father's round cursive but in square, neat printing. I wondered if Zoey liked the idea of being a journalist's wife, and how her snazzy car looked parked outside a ramshackle house in the hills of California, the kind of house that a writer like my father would have chosen.

All these thoughts were tumbling around in my head, but I didn't speak except to read the directions aloud to Charlie while Sam fiddled with the radio. Charlie remained silent too, until we tore a hole in the wall of fog halfway across the Golden Gate Bridge.

"Interesting," Charlie said, and smiled slightly.

"Are you *kidding*?" I said. I would have punched him in the arm if he hadn't been driving.

The water was a sparkling sheet of midnight-blue far below. Ahead, the hills of Marin County (according to Patrick's directions, or, rather, Zoey's) boldly rose from the waves. I rolled down the window, which I had rolled up against the surprising summer chill of San Francisco, and took a deep breath of damp, briny air.

The smell reminded me of home. It was like the Connecticut shore but wetter. It was a comforting smell.

Then we were over the bridge and plunging down onto Bridgeway Boulevard and into Sausalito.

"Good grief," I murmured. It looked like one of those small New England towns that tourists love, except this one was California style: shops and restaurants and drifting crowds of people and charming buildings that looked old and new at the same time. Only I knew that these had to be all new. California towns haven't been around *that* long.

Charlie edged through town and turned left. The road wound slightly upward into the hills. But the houses we saw weren't shacks. They were glass-and-cedar constructions, nestling in jungles of carefully tended flowers.

"Good grief," I said again. Suddenly, I didn't think Patrick lived in a shack anymore.

And I was right.

❋ Chapter 6

"Whoa," said Sam, switching off the radio as we pulled up to one side of the cedar, stone, and glass structure that could have come from the pages of a very expensive magazine. The house was set on a slight hill. We followed a path from the car to the back door (the one for which we had the key), past a rock garden filled with ferns and hostas (which I recognized from Watson's and Nannie's gardens) and tiny creeping plants with flowers like stars. Up ahead, a little waterfall trickled down into a pool. Glancing up, I saw that one of the big back windows looked down at the waterfall. A deck wrapped partway around the house. In one place a huge old tree was growing up through the middle of it. Although the house obviously wasn't very old, it looked as if it belonged in the setting, unlike a lot of the big, fancy houses in my hometown. The place felt serene and calm.

Did Patrick really live *here*?

We let ourselves into an enormous room with tall ceilings and a flood of light.

"Wow," I said.

"He appears to have done okay for himself," Charlie grumbled.

I gave Charlie a Look.

We dumped our bags by the door. Sam said, suddenly, "I'm thirsty," and made a beeline for the state-of-the-art stainless steel refrigerator nestled in one corner of the room.

"Sam," I began.

"Hey, the letter said to make ourselves at home," Sam replied, opening a glass-fronted cabinet and setting a glass on the slate countertop. He opened the huge, sleek refrigerator and filled the glass with orange juice. "Anyone else want some?"

"No, thanks," I said.

Charlie shook his head. He was examining the sound system in one corner of the room. I saw his eyes go to the speakers.

I noted that the plants had followed us inside. Several of them reached up toward the sun streaming through the broad windows. On a small table, a cluster of cacti of every shape and color bristled. I tried to imagine Patrick tending to the plants. I knew that cacti didn't need to be watered much, but even so, I couldn't see it.

To one side, a hall led to four small rooms. One pair of rooms was joined by a bathroom. At the end of the hall, a larger room was obviously a study, with a scarred desk buried beneath a computer, a printer, a jumble of paper, and some books. More books were stacked all over the floor, and pictures of Willie Mays, Cynthia Cooper, Babe Didrickson Zaharias, and Lou Gehrig (that famous photograph taken on his last day in baseball) were thumbtacked to the walls and a bulletin board. Across the hall, next to a half bath, was another room. This one was neat as a pin, but it too had a desk, a computer, and a printer. Here, there were orderly rows of bookshelves.

Zoey's? I went in and found a photograph on the desk: a strongly built woman of about my father's age — and just as tall as he was — standing next to my father with the ocean behind them and far below.

I put the photograph back and returned to what I thought was my father's study. But I saw no photographs except those of the sports stars.

When I returned to the living room, Charlie was walking down the stairs that curled up to the gallery above. "This joint is huge. It doesn't look it, but it is," he said, and his tone sounded disapproving somehow. "There's a gigantic bedroom with a deck back there," he motioned toward the end of the gallery, above where I'd been exploring, "and two more rooms and a bath along the gallery."

"Two studies, two bedrooms," I reported, nodding in the direction from which I'd come. I wandered over to a low bookshelf and bent to examine the photographs on top of it.

I recognized Patrick right away, of course. And I recognized the woman standing next to him from the photo I'd seen on her desk. Her head was turned and she was smiling at someone to one side of the photograph. Patrick's arms were around her and she was grinning a megawatt grin.

The woman was in several other photographs with Patrick too: standing next to what looked like a recently planted tree, with a group of friends on someone's deck, perched on the steps of a building. She *had* to be Zoey, I concluded. To my surprise, I realized I was relieved. Zoey looked friendly and nice and, well, reliable. Her hair was light brown streaked with blonde and what might have been the beginnings of gray, and she wore it short. In fact, I noticed that Patrick's hair was as long as hers.

Patrick looked like a solid citizen too, I had to admit. I noticed that several of the photographs had been taken in front of the same restaurant and in one of those shots, Patrick was wearing an apron.

"Hey," I said. "Check this out." Sam and then Charlie appeared at my side. "He's wearing an apron," I pointed out. "You think he got a new job or something?"

"Cooking?" Charlie's eyebrows went up.

"No way," said Sam. "He's a sportswriter, remember? It was probably just some party."

Remembering the cluttered study with the faces of famous athletes looking down from the walls, I had to agree.

Charlie added, "Yeah. It's the one thing he's been consistent about. His dedication to his career as a sportswriter."

As if on cue, the back door opened. The three of us turned as Patrick walked into the house and back into our lives.

"You're here," he said as if he were somehow surprised. He stopped and stared at us. He was holding a shopping bag.

I put the photograph down. My brain registered

that the woman from the other pictures stood right behind him and that she was holding a shopping bag too.

Nobody moved or said anything for a long moment. Then Zoey crossed the room, set her shopping bag down, returned and took the shopping bag from Patrick, and gave him a little push with her free hand.

He walked across the room toward us. I started forward too. When I reached my father, I hugged him. In fact, I hugged him a lot harder than he hugged me. He seemed tentative, unsure of himself. When he let go, he turned, and I realized that Sam was standing next to me.

"Well," Patrick said. "Sam."

Another pause, and then Patrick held out his hand, and he and Sam shook hands. It wasn't a particularly fatherly gesture, but I thought Sam seemed a little relieved.

Next, Patrick turned to Charlie, who, I was glad to see, had joined us. But Charlie didn't reach out to return the handshake Patrick offered. Instead, he said coolly, "Hello."

Patrick smiled. He stepped back. "Let me look at you," he said. "It's been so long."

"Whose fault is that?" said Charlie. His voice had gone from cool to cold.

Patrick's cheeks reddened. Uh-oh. I tried to think of something to say.

The woman stepped forward and smiled at us. "I've been looking forward to meeting you," she said. "I've heard so much about you."

I sensed rather than saw Charlie open his mouth, ready to take another shot at Patrick. But he didn't get a chance.

Beaming, my father put his arm around the woman. He said proudly, "Sam, Charlie, Kristy, this is Zoey Amberson. She's about to become my new wife."

✽ Chapter 7

My new wife. How strange that sounded. How deeply weird.

This would make Zoey my stepmother.

That and a million other thoughts rushed through my mind as I stepped forward and held out my hand. "I'm glad to meet you," I said. We shook hands.

She smiled and the creases on the sides of her mouth deepened into dimples. "I'm glad to meet you too, Kristy. Call me Zoey."

She shook hands with Sam and Charlie, and I was relieved to see that Charlie was polite and even smiled at her. At least he wasn't transferring his anger at Patrick onto an innocent bystander.

And then I thought about those words — *innocent bystander* — and wondered if Zoey knew just how unreliable Patrick was. She'd said she'd heard a lot about us, but what had she heard? What had Patrick told her about the family he walked out on? How was he going to explain the awkwardness of this meeting, Sam's formality, Charlie's hostility?

When we'd finished saying hello, Patrick looked at his watch. "Anybody hungry? After that plane ride and the airplane food, you should be. And it's past lunchtime here."

Somewhat to my surprise, I realized that I was.

I nodded and Sam said, "Sure."

Charlie shrugged.

If Patrick noticed, he gave no sign. He and Zoey were already moving toward the kitchen. With team-like precision that seemed to suggest they often worked together, they began to unpack the two bags they'd set on the counter.

"Sandwiches would be fine," I said. "Don't go to any trouble."

Patrick grinned. "It's no trouble. We brought this from the Greenhouse."

"The greenhouse? A plant place?" asked Sam.

"No. It's a restaurant," said Zoey. "With lots of plants and great food." She gave my father a fond look. "Especially now that we have the right chef."

As she spoke, she unwrapped plates and lined

them up on the counter. Patrick took ingredients out of the refrigerator and began to chop something.

"Can I help?" I asked.

"We'll sit at the counter," said Zoey. "Patrick and I have already eaten, but we'll have coffee with you. Why don't you set out plates and glasses and silverware?"

Relieved not to be idle, I took charge, giving Charlie the silverware so he'd have to do something other than stand there and glower. I assigned Sam the job of getting glasses and filling them with ice and water.

"Very organized," Patrick observed.

"It's something Kristy is famous for," Charlie said. "Everyone who knows her knows that."

"I seem to remember that she had definite ideas about the way things worked," Patrick said easily. He smiled at me and continued. "Not like her old man. But I've improved with age. One of the first rules of cooking is 'clean up as you go along.' "

I couldn't remember ever seeing Patrick in the kitchen. But now he moved with assurance. In no time at all we were sitting in front of plates heaped with salad and what Patrick called California chicken sandwiches, made with grilled chicken and homemade mayonnaise on dark, rosemary-scented bread. The salad had avocado and something called jicama and all kinds of different lettuces that I didn't recognize. The dressing, Zoey told us, was the Greenhouse special dressing.

It was awfully fancy for a "simple" lunch, and it was delicious.

"When did you learn to cook?" asked Charlie. I wondered if he'd also tried to remember Patrick in the kitchen and failed.

"Yeah. This is decent. It was nice of you to stop by the restaurant and pick it up for us," Sam said.

"No problem," said Zoey. "It's my restaurant."

"And I'm not just a good cook now, I'm the chef," Patrick added.

"Chef," I repeated blankly.

"Chef," Patrick said. "You know, those guys with white hats that you see on television. Only I don't wear the white hat."

"At the restaurant?" I asked. "The Greenhouse?"

"That's the one. I know the boss." He smiled at Zoey.

"I thought you were a sportswriter," Sam said, forgetting he was still chewing a bite of sandwich.

Patrick shrugged. "I changed my mind. Oh, I still do a little freelance writing, but my career wasn't exactly big-time."

Charlie didn't say anything.

"It wasn't my idea, actually," Patrick said. "I did an article on a football player who had wrecked his knees and gone to the Culinary Institute of America out here. One thing led to another and the next thing I know, I'm in cooking school at night, just for the heck of it. That's when I met Zoey. She was taking a restaurant management course."

We'd finished lunch. Zoey jumped to her feet. "Why don't you show everyone to their rooms, Patrick, and I'll clean up. Then we can take a little tour of Sausalito."

Sausalito, Zoey told us, had started out as a little fishing village. Now it was every bit the bustling tourist town that it looked, but it was still fun to walk around and see the sights. And Patrick made an excellent tour guide. We ended the afternoon at the Greenhouse, which was set back on a hill just above the town. We drank mugs of mochaccino with whipped cream, and even Charlie seemed to relax. He talked easily enough to Zoey about school and his car.

But he fell silent when Patrick proudly showed off the kitchen and introduced us to the sous-chef,

Juanita Alvarez, who was there checking on deliveries.

"What does a sous-chef do, exactly?" I asked.

"It's like being the assistant chef," said Juanita. "I'm in charge of cutting things up, getting ingredients ready, stuff like that."

"Tonight you're the chef in charge," Patrick said. "Don't forget."

"I won't," Juanita said. Someone pushed through the back door with an enormous stack of boxes labeled CERTIFIED ORGANIC, and Juanita began flipping through the papers on her clipboard. "Welcome to California," she called over her shoulder as she took the invoice from the delivery person.

"We're having dinner a little late tonight," said Zoey. "I'm going to stay at the restaurant for awhile. I'll be home about eight or so, when things start to slow down, and we'll eat then."

"Sounds good," I said. The more I was around Zoey, the more I liked her — even though I felt vaguely guilty about it. But I wasn't going to think about that now.

We offered to help with dinner, but after he let us set the table, Patrick sent us out to explore the winding roads of his neighborhood. We walked on the wide gravel shoulder because there weren't any sidewalks. Most of the time, we only knew where houses were by the mailboxes at the end of curved driveways. The houses themselves were set back among the trees, out of sight.

We walked without talking much, whether from tiredness or a sense of being overwhelmed, it was hard to say. When the sun was beginning to go down, we headed back to Patrick's house. As we trudged up the back steps, we could see the table, candles glowing softly. Harp music was playing, and Zoey's car was back.

Patrick looked up as we walked in. "Perfect timing," he said. "Wash your hands, then dinner is served."

The table was massive and round. Patrick sat in the chair closest to the kitchen. Zoey insisted on taking the chair with its back to the window, so that the rest of us could enjoy the view.

"Maybe one day this week we'll go into San Francisco," she told us as we ate.

"Cool," said Sam.

We were silent for a little while, concentrating on the elegant dinner Patrick had prepared. "This is good," I offered at last.

"Pasta primavera," said Patrick. "Simple and basic and good for you."

"It looks like pasta with a bunch of vegetables," Sam said.

"Got it in one," Patrick answered. "That's what it is."

Looking around the table, I couldn't help comparing this with the family dinner we'd had the week before, the one that Patrick's phone call had interrupted. The noise of conversation and the chink of plates and forks and the easy informality back home contrasted sharply with the candlelit table at which I now sat, where everyone — or almost everyone — seemed to be on their best behavior. The only thing the two meals had in common was food with an unfamiliar name.

"We have a lot to do before this Saturday," Zoey said. "Unless you guys brought your own tuxedos."

"Tuxedos," repeated Sam in a horrified voice. He turned accusing eyes toward Patrick. "You didn't say anything about tuxedos."

Patrick laughed. "Well, it's going to be a formal wedding, small but elegant. Six o'clock in the evening . . . so I want you guys to have tuxes, and Kristy, Zoey'll take you shopping for a smashing new dress."

"A new dress?" I croaked, caught by surprise. "But I brought a dress." I didn't add that I'd brought my only dress. Who needs more than one?

But Patrick didn't pay me any heed. He rolled on, full of plans. "*And* I need you two guys to give me moral support. I haven't even rented a tux for *me* yet."

I studied Patrick as he talked. He was being majorly charming. He launched into a story about a borrowed tuxedo that he'd worn to an awards ceremony, and how he'd split the seat of the pants right before he'd had to go up on the stage. I couldn't help but laugh. Charlie even grinned a little. Patrick was working hard to put us all at ease, to make us enjoy ourselves — and to make us like him. Was this a new Patrick I was seeing? Or was it the same old Patrick who had walked out on his family without seeming to care at all? He'd been charming then too, I remembered.

"Plus, I have another announcement," Patrick said, looking like a self-important little kid.

"Now?" Zoey began. "Oh, Patrick, do you think . . ."

His eyes flashed with annoyance and I saw the corners of his mouth go down. "Yes, I do, Zoey," he said, like a brat.

That was another side of Patrick I remembered as well, that quick sharpness whenever he didn't get his way or when, as a child, I'd been slow to understand what he'd been trying to teach me.

Just as suddenly, the moment of temper was gone and Patrick was grinning broadly. "I want you guys, Sam, Charlie, to be my best men at the wedding. I know it's a little unusual to have two, but hey, you're my sons."

What about David Michael? I wondered. Patrick had a third son. Had he forgotten?

Sam said, "Really? What do we have to do?"

"Stand with me in front of the minister, make sure I don't faint or lose the ring. And look terrific in your tuxes."

"Cool," said Sam. "I'm in."

"No," said Charlie flatly. "You'll have to make do with only one of your *three* sons."

Charlie had not forgotten David Michael either.

He took another bite of pasta and chewed fiercely. We all stared at him.

I saw that flash of anger in my father's face again. Zoey intervened before he could speak. "Are you sure, Charlie? Why don't you think about it before you make a decision?"

Deliberately, Charlie put down his fork. He

pushed his chair back and stood up. His face was stern, and once again he looked much older than his seventeen years.

Patrick had regained a grip on his temper. He said, "Hey, do your old man a favor, will you? I promise I won't ask you to do it again."

"No," said Charlie. I saw Patrick's eyes narrow. But I also saw the hurt look that crossed his face.

"Charlie," he said, in a softer, almost pleading voice.

Charlie said, "What right do you have to ask me to be your best man? You left when I was ten, in case you've forgotten. I don't know you. You don't know me. Asking me to be your best man isn't going to make us good buddies. And it's not going to make you into the father you've never been to me. Or to Sam or David Michael, in case you've forgotten him."

"That's enough!" Patrick said, no trace of pleading or sadness in his voice now. "Your behavior is way out of line."

"No, it's not," said Charlie. "You're the one who behaved badly. But of course that probably slipped your mind." He dropped his napkin by his plate and stomped down the hall to the bedroom.

✳ Chapter 8

Charlie was making a habit of stomping away from the dinner table, I thought drowsily as I woke up the next morning. But Zoey had been cool about it. She'd said, "Well, give him time and some space. Maybe he'll change his mind," and then she had changed the subject. Sam and I had followed her lead and soon I'd found myself genuinely interested in her descriptions of life in the restaurant business.

Patrick had not taken it so easily. He showed his anger throughout dinner, remaining tight-lipped and monosyllabic in his answers when we tried to include him in the conversation. It wasn't until dessert that he had loosened up again.

I climbed out of bed and peered out my window. Wow, what a gloomy day, I thought. Only then did I catch a glimpse of silvery pink, low on the horizon, and realize how early it must be. Glancing at my watch, I saw that it was 8:30 in the morning Stoneybrook time, but only 5:30 A.M. Sausalito time. The thought that I was actually up at such an amazingly early hour suddenly made me sleepy. Yawning so hugely I thought my jaws would crack, I crawled back into bed.

When I awoke again, it was to the sound of a voice, loud and off-key, singing, "Time to shop, time to shop, time to sho-o-o-o-op!" A moment later, I heard a tap on my door and then Zoey's voice saying, "Kristy? Time to wake up."

Downstairs, I found Patrick, Zoey, Charlie, and Sam. Zoey smiled at me over the cup of coffee she was cradling in her hands. "Charlie tells me that you're not much for dresses," she said.

"Uh," I replied. "Well . . ."

"Nonsense," said Patrick. "What woman doesn't like to shop for clothes?"

"Plenty of women, Patrick," said Zoey. "In fact, you spend more time shopping for clothes than I do, in case you hadn't noticed."

Wow. Zoey didn't take any guff from Patrick, I thought. I expected to see the quick snap of anger in his eyes, especially when Sam gave a muffled snort.

But Patrick only grinned at Zoey, and all I could see in his eyes was affection. "Possibly you are right. Who am I to argue with so beautiful a lady?"

Zoey rolled her eyes and then said to me, "Don't worry, Kristy. We'll make this as quick and painless as possible."

Charlie declined to join us, as I had known he would. "You don't have to look at tuxes," Patrick urged. "Do a little sightseeing."

"Thanks," said Charlie. "But I want to catch up on my reading."

"Reading?" said Sam, looking at Charlie as if he had dropped in from Mars. He and I both knew that the only things Charlie ever read were *The Sporting News* and the sports pages of the newspaper.

"My summer reading," said Charlie.

"You brought a book with you?" Sam persisted.

Charlie reddened. Before he could answer, Zoey said, "Well, if you get bored with your book, we have plenty of others. Help yourself."

"Thanks," said Charlie. He added, somewhat grudgingly, "Have fun."

To my surprise, I did. When we reached the shops of Sausalito, Patrick insisted we "synchronize watches." We agreed to meet back at the house in two hours (and I tried not to groan out loud at the prospect of shopping, *for a dress,* for two whole hours). Then Zoey and I were off.

I'd opted for jeans and a long-sleeved shirt, tucked in, the neat but casual statement. Zoey was wearing baggy khaki pants and a bright green crocheted vest over a yellow-and-blue-striped cotton chemise. Heavy espadrilles with colorful ribbons were on her feet. Her only jewelry was a ring with a small, square-cut emerald that hung on a gold chain around her neck. It was a look that suited her and showed a flair that reminded me of Claudia, the fashion arbiter and designer of the BSC.

Our first stop was a fancy dress shop. "Nothing pink or blue for you," Zoey said immediately, to my relief. "And you need a simple line, I think. A slip dress, maybe, but with a little more substance."

"Okay," I said. These were the sorts of words that Claudia and Stacey, a New York fashion statement herself, sometimes tossed around at BSC meetings. I just hoped a slip dress didn't mean I would be going around in my underwear like last year's rock star.

I won't say it was easy, exactly. I mean, I was totally embarrassed when I got stuck in one dress that wrapped and tied in about six places. I couldn't figure out how to finish tying it, and I couldn't untie it either.

After a long struggle during which, fortunately, I didn't rip anything, I gave up. "Help," I yelled from the dressing room.

No one answered. Would I have to lurch out into the store, tied up like a Christmas gift reject?

"Help!" I yelled again, more loudly.

"Kristy?"

"Zoey," I said. "Could you give me a hand in here?"

The dressing room door opened. To her credit, Zoey didn't laugh. But I could see the smile in her eyes.

"If you get me out of this thing, you can laugh," I told her.

"Okay," said Zoey. She unwound me, then sat down on the little stool in the dressing room and roared.

I had to laugh too. It *was* pretty funny.

Fortunately, we weren't tied up in dress shopping much longer (ha-ha). In fact, with Zoey's expert guidance, we found a dress at the second shop we went to. And it was velvety (wow — even I was impressed), colored a deep burgundy. And it didn't look like a slip to me, with its regular neckline, right at my collarbone, and short sleeves that showed off my tanned arms. Zoey complimented me on them. "Strong," she observed. "With good muscles. I know women who exercise madly to have arms like that."

"Oh," I said, embarrassed. "Well, I do exercise a lot, I guess. I mean, I like to play softball."

We agreed that the dress was perfect, and before I knew it, I was standing on the sidewalk a free woman. Well, practically. Zoey said we still had to find some shoes but declared that we deserved a break first.

We strolled through the town and I thought about the fact that, so far, shopping hadn't been as painful an ordeal as I had expected. I liked Zoey more and more.

We found a seat on the wharf overlooking the water and sat down. Zoey stretched her legs out and said, "This is *such* a luxury. Sometimes I feel as if I'm on my feet twenty-four/seven at the restaurant." Her hand went up to the ring on the gold chain and she slid it back and forth absently.

"That's a nice ring," I said.

She smiled. "My engagement ring. I wear it on a

chain because I got out of the habit of wearing rings after I lost a few zillion of them by taking them off and putting them down while I worked in kitchens. At least one was kneaded into bread dough and was never seen again." She looked down at the ring. "It is beautiful, isn't it? Your father has excellent taste, if I do say so myself."

"I guess," I said, not sure what to say.

Zoey turned to look at me. "This situation can't be easy for you, Kristy."

"Uh, well," I said. "I guess not. I mean, not exactly."

"You know what? My father has been married four times." She laughed. "You could say, in one sense, that he's the marrying kind. He just had his fourth wedding a few months ago."

"Did you go?"

"I catered it," said Zoey. "It turned out to be fun, in a weird way. But I'll tell you, even when you hit forty, it isn't easy seeing your dad marrying a woman who isn't your mom, no matter how nice she is."

Although I liked Zoey, I wasn't ready to pour out my heart to her or anything. So I just said, "It is a little strange."

"I'm glad you came," Zoey said simply.

I said, "Me too," and mostly meant it. We sat in

the sun in comfortable silence for a long time. Then Zoey looked at her watch. "Shoes," she said.

"No heels," I warned her.

"A sensible decision," Zoey agreed, cementing my opinion that shopping — with her, anyway — wasn't so bad after all.

And maybe the wedding wouldn't be either.

❊ Chapter 9

We beat Patrick and Sam home. Charlie was lounging on the deck in a hammock, actually reading a book. It was a paperback called *Willie's Time,* with a picture of Willie Mays on the cover.

"I guess the book you brought wasn't too good," I said pointedly. "How's that one?"

Charlie had the grace to blush. "Pretty good," he said. "I found it in the study."

I noticed that he avoided saying Patrick's name — or calling him Dad.

"Charles Einstein is a good writer," said Zoey. "I like reading baseball history. One of my favorites is *The Glory of Their Times*. It's a collection of interviews with some of the early players of the game."

To my complete shock, Charlie's eyes lit up. "A classic," he said. "That is the coolest book."

"I'm going to hang up my dress," I announced.

When I returned, Zoey and Charlie were deep in a discussion of books and sportswriters. "And Robert Lipsyte is another great sportswriter," I heard Charlie declare. "He was one of the first writers to recognize Ali for the boxing star he was."

"You're more than the average sports fan," Zoey said. "Not many fans can talk about the writing that goes with the games."

Charlie made a face. "Hey, the sports announcers are so dim, you have to read, or all you'd know is a lot of meaningless computer-generated stats."

I said, without thinking, "That's right. You and Patrick used to watch baseball games with the sound off and the radio on. And you still do, Charlie."

Charlie froze and I could have bitten my tongue. Me and my big mouth.

Zoey said, "Patrick still does that also. Sometimes I think he would have been happiest as a radio sports announcer."

"Can we use the cappuccino machine?" I jumped in.

"Sure," said Zoey. "I'll show you how. Then you can make coffee for Patrick when he and Sam get back. Shopping can be so exhausting."

"Well, I'll shop with you anytime," I said.

Zoey gave me her deep-dimpled grin and I could tell she was pleased. "Thanks, Kristy." She went on, easily, "You know, the fact that you guys are here means a lot to both of us, especially Patrick. He is *so* pleased and proud."

"Then why can't he tell us that himself?" Charlie asked. He spoke in a low voice and it was clear that he wasn't trying to be mean or nasty, or even defensive.

Zoey didn't try to give him an answer. She only said, "I don't know, Charlie. He *should* tell you himself."

After that, Charlie and I focused on mastering the cappuccino machine. It wasn't very hard.

And then Patrick and Sam came home. They were positively beaming with pride. "We came, we saw, we shopped," Patrick announced.

"You wouldn't believe the tuxedos out here," said Sam. "They make the ones I've seen back home look totally lame."

"So what did you pick out?" I asked.

"We looked in about a million places," said Sam. "And then we went to The Tuxedo Cat and found the perfect tuxedos for all three of us. The Tuxedo

Cat is cool. This actual cat lives in the store, and he's black with white markings so he looks like he's wearing a tuxedo. And his name is Tuxedo."

Although I had a definitely decent dress, I was suddenly a little envious — until Patrick pulled out a brochure, opened it, and spread it, with a flourish, on the counter. "Ta-da," he said. "With a few alterations, we're going to be amazing."

Zoey, Charlie, and I stared in stupefaction at the photos of the tuxedos Sam and Patrick had chosen.

"Amazing," I echoed in a weak voice.

They were the ugliest tuxedos in the history of the world. I hadn't known it was possible for a tuxedo to look so bad. But these did. They were a sort of unnatural yellow-orange that, for one thing, was going to clash with my new dress. Even I could tell that. And ruffled shirts, with matching yellow-orange edging? I don't think so.

Charlie didn't hesitate. He said, "No way I'm putting that on and wearing it in public. It is hands-down ugly."

"Hey," said Patrick. "You had your chance to go shopping with us."

"If I'd been shopping with you and I'd seen that, I'd have run screaming out of the store. It could star in a horror movie," Charlie said.

I choked back a snicker. He was right.

"Try not to ruin the fun, okay, Charlie?" said Patrick, his eyes snapping with anger.

"I'm afraid Charlie is right," Zoey said calmly. "They are truly, deeply awful. What were you thinking, Patrick?"

"Hey! These are great tuxes. Kristy, tell them." Patrick and Sam looked at me expectantly. I could see the laughter in Sam's eyes and could tell he wasn't bugged by the criticism. For a fleeting moment, I wondered if he'd deliberately egged Patrick on to pick out the ugliest tuxedos in the world.

I took a deep breath. I let them have the truth. "Ugly," I pronounced. "With a capital *U*."

"What?" Patrick's voice almost blew the roof off.

"Three against two, Patrick. You lose," Zoey said. "Coffee, anyone?"

"I *like* these tuxes and so does Sam. We're not changing our minds."

Zoey said, "You can wear those tuxes if you want. Just not to our wedding."

"*Our* wedding. That's right. I have a say in this too," sputtered Patrick.

"Baby-puke yellow," I said, suddenly, identifying a color all too familiar to baby-sitters everywhere.

"What?" Patrick turned to me.

"The color. That's what color those tuxes are," I said.

Charlie and Zoey both laughed.

Patrick didn't. "Very funny," he said.

"Come on, Patrick. It is kind of funny," said Zoey. "Besides, it means you get to shop some more."

Patrick glared at the rest of us. Sam ducked his head. Then Patrick said, "Fine. We'll reconsider our decision. But only if Charlie goes with us."

"Okay," said Charlie, to my surprise.

And that was that, except for the mystery of how my father, a man who was supposed to have good taste, could have chosen such incredibly awful tuxedos in the first place.

The next day, we all went to The Tuxedo Cat. Patrick was *not* on his best behavior. He sulked. As Sam and Zoey pulled out tuxedos and flipped through books, he kept saying, "Whatever," in a bored voice.

Sam commented on every tuxedo, glancing from Patrick to Zoey like a spectator at a tennis match. "What about this?" he'd say, showing a tux to Zoey. Then he'd turn to Patrick. "This would be cool," he'd say encouragingly. He reminded me of me, trying to sweet-talk a difficult baby-sitting charge into behaving.

I pitched in and even held up a few tuxedos against myself to admire the effect in the three-way mirror. Princess Diana, the late fashion-great (that's what my friend Claudia calls her, anyway), had been photographed decked out in a tuxedo. Maybe I'd try the look myself one day.

But after Patrick had said "Whatever," for about the umpteenth time, Zoey got fed up. She put her hands on her hips, gave Patrick a long, level stare, and said, "Patrick, you're picking out tuxedos to wear in *our* wedding. Are you in or are you out?"

Looking from one to the other, I had the feeling that Zoey was talking about more than just the tuxedo. I found myself holding my breath, waiting for his answer.

Patrick glowered at Zoey. Then he glanced at Charlie. Charlie's face was stony. Patrick looked at Sam, but Sam had looked away, his attention apparently riveted on a rack of shirts. Finally Patrick glanced at me. The sulky expression eased and he dropped one eyelid in a slight wink.

Then he rolled his eyes and heaved a big, theatrical sigh. "Really, Zoey, they're just tuxedos. I bow to your superior taste." It was a little sarcastic, but then he smiled and threw his arms around her in a bear hug and lifted her up. When he put her down, they were both laughing.

I let my breath out. Charlie rolled *his* eyes, and I could tell that he thought Patrick had gotten off too easily. Sam looked visibly relieved.

After that, things went more smoothly. By the time we strolled back out onto Bridgeway Boulevard to check up on the flower arrangements, everything seemed fine.

Patrick and Zoey introduced us to the florist, who provided fresh flowers for the Greenhouse. The three of them fell into a discussion involving baby's breath, herbal essences and their effect on social situations (whatever that meant), and the color scheme for the wedding (which did *not* include baby-puke yellow, although Patrick did get his way about yellow roses as boutonnieres for himself and Sam and Charlie).

It was a discussion worthy of Nannie and Watson, and I found my mind drifting back to the preparations for Mom and Watson's wedding. We had had more than a few difficulties. After all, not only was our mom remarrying, but we were acquiring a whole new family *and* moving to a new house. In addition, I'd been convinced that Watson was way too uptight and formal. I mean, here was a guy who said "resume your seat" instead of "sit back down" to his kids at the dinner table. I tried to tell myself he was okay, if he made Mom happy, but I thought he could be a stiff, stubborn jerk sometimes.

But that had passed. We survived the wedding and even had fun, and now I wouldn't trade my large, blended, noisy family — and especially Watson — for anything.

Patrick and Zoey weren't combining families. Having the three of us show up for the wedding didn't count as a combination platter. We weren't going to have to move to a new place or change much of anything.

So what was the problem? Why was this wedding so much more difficult to deal with than Mom and Watson's?

I didn't understand it, especially considering that I liked Zoey much more, upon knowing her for only a couple of days, than I had liked Watson. Figuring this out made me feel a little guilty, I can tell you. It was as if I were somehow betraying Watson, even though I knew I wasn't, because I loved him so much more now.

I watched as Patrick chose a single rose, bowed, and presented it to Zoey. She took it, snapped the stem, and pinned the flower to the shoulder of her dress.

We headed back to the car. Our next stop would be a quick one, to the veranda at the back of the old Italian-style hotel where the wedding ceremony was going to be held.

"The view is wonderful," Patrick said. "The finest in Sausalito. After that, we'll finish the grand tour of the town. I'll even show you where I used to live, over in Waldo Point Harbor Houseboats."

"You lived on a houseboat?" Sam said, and this time the enthusiasm wasn't strained, as it had been when we'd been shopping for tuxes.

"Of course," said Patrick. "It's where we creative types like to live. The freedom of the open seas." He made a face and he and Sam began to talk about houseboats and boats.

Zoey, who was driving, caught my eye in the mirror and smiled, and I realized another unsettling thing about this whole wedding business.

Not only did I like Zoey but, as charming as Patrick was now being, I liked her better than my own father right now.

What did *that* mean?

❋ Chapter 10

"This was a bad idea," Charlie said. "I want to leave."

"We can't," I answered. He and I were leaning over the rail of the Sausalito ferry, on our way back from the Angel Island Wildlife Preserve. Sam was somewhere nearby, but I hadn't seen him or Patrick for awhile.

It had not been a perfect day. The picnic trip to Angel Island had been Zoey's idea, and I could tell by Patrick's surprised and not entirely pleased look that he hadn't been enthusiastic. Zoey hadn't appeared to notice when she'd brought it up that morning, shortly before departing for the restaurant.

"We've had such fun there, Patrick," she said encouragingly. "You can kick back, take some time off from the wedding planning, catch up on what's been happening since you were all together last."

I saw Charlie give Zoey a funny look. I admit, I was thinking the same thing I was pretty sure he was thinking: Just how much had Patrick told Zoey about his, well, ex-family? Did she know it had been more than six years since we'd all been together?

Patrick said, "I'm sure the kids have other things they'd much rather do."

Like what? I wondered. We were strangers in Sausalito as well as in Patrick's life.

"Take them with you, Zoey," Patrick went on. "Let them explore Sausalito some more. I'll catch up on some things I need to do, and then for lunch I'll come meet you guys."

"Things?" Zoey gave him a Look. "Windsurfing things?"

Patrick looked sheepish. "Well, it *has* been a long time since I've been out."

Windsurfing? Patrick? I couldn't decide if it was cool or weird that someone my father's age was out there on a board.

Picking up her keys, Zoey said, "Take a Frisbee. In fact, I'll tell you what. If you stop by the restaurant, I'll have a first-class picnic lunch ready for you."

Patrick gave in, but I could tell he wasn't entirely happy.

So we ended up on Angel Island. Zoey hadn't been kidding — the picnic had been first-class. And the weather was perfect. We watched birds through the binoculars. Sam swore he saw a shark's fin, far out on the water, and then Patrick entertained us with stories of people-shark encounters in California.

When that topic had been exhausted, he turned to Charlie, who'd been almost entirely silent, and said, "So, Chuck. Tell me what's been going on. Bring me up to speed."

Charlie gave Patrick a level look. "No one calls me Chuck, for one thing," he said. "I'm going to college next year. I was in fifth grade when you walked out. In spite of everything, Mom's been great, and Watson is going to help pay for my college education."

Whoa. Sam's eyes widened and I let out a little gasp.

Patrick said, "I don't think I like your tone."

Charlie just looked at him.

Sam jumped up, grabbed the Frisbee, and said, "You're it," to me. He winged it in my direction. I jumped up too, and we took off down the beach.

When we came back, Charlie's figure was just a

speck on the shoreline and Patrick was leaning back on his elbows, his dark glasses on, his face turned to the sun.

We caught the next ferry back. At first, Patrick focused all his attention on me. Sam was cutting up outrageously, trying to get Patrick's attention, or maybe trying to keep Charlie from saying anything else. At last I announced that I was going to the bathroom. Returning, I found Charlie leaning against the rail, and I settled in next to him to watch the waves slip by.

"If we leave now," I said, "it'll ruin everything."

"Not for Patrick," Charlie said. "But I guess it would for Zoey." He paused, then said, "What does she see in him anyway?"

I shrugged.

"You *would* defend him," Charlie went on. "He's made it pretty obvious you're his favorite."

What could I say to that? I shrugged again.

"How do you think that makes me feel? Or Sam?"

"What am I supposed to do?"

Now it was Charlie's turn to shrug. Then he said, "Don't be taken in by him, Kristy, that's all."

"I won't," I said. And then I wondered, Is that

what had happened to Zoey? Had she been taken in?

Is that what had happened to Mom?

We arrived home to find a message from Zoey. I had to laugh (and so did Sam and Charlie) at the look on Patrick's face as he played back the tape. "Patrick. We have a few more members of my family arriving tomorrow, I'm afraid. Not only is my mom coming, but Dad is bringing his new wife. And his other two ex-wives, Mona and Ariel, have called to say they're joining us too. Could you call around and find them a nice place to stay — but put all the ex-wives in separate hotels. They really don't get along. Thanks."

"Great," said Patrick. "And Jeannie, Zoey's mom, is coming with *her* mother, Mrs. Argos, who practically spits nails when she sees Zoey's father."

"This would make a great movie," said Sam. "Really funny."

"Somehow, I'm not laughing," said Patrick. But he did grin.

Zoey came home and congratulated Patrick when he told her he'd put Mona in the Casa Madrone Hotel and sent Ariel to a harborside bed-and-breakfast at a safe distance. The rest of the family was staying at the Alta Mira Hotel, where the wedding was being held, except for Zoey's mother and grandmother, who were staying with Jessica Sara Klein, Zoey's best friend and bridesmaid. Jessica lived in the nearby town of Mill Valley.

Before dinner, Sam, Charlie, and I gave Mom and Watson another call (we'd also called them when we'd gotten to the airport). It was strange to hear our Stoneybrook world was still going on while we were in California. After dinner, Zoey took out two sheets of paper and spread them on the table. They looked a little like blueprints, but they were filled with circles and had clearly been written on and erased a lot. "The seating arrangements," she explained.

Patrick groaned.

Charlie leaned forward. "The seating arrangements for what?"

"The rehearsal dinner and the wedding. There are some people who should sit together," Zoey said.

"And some who definitely shouldn't," Patrick finished for her. "Fortunately for me, Ray isn't coming."

I'd forgotten about Ray, our uncle and Patrick's only brother. (Their parents — my grandparents — had died before I was born.) I gave Patrick a puzzled look. Patrick shrugged. "We had a disagreement, and when I sent Ray an invitation, he sent back best wishes but said no way."

That's when it hit me. We were Dad's only family at the wedding. Before I could think about that, Zoey was handing Patrick a list and a pen. "Here's the guest list. When I call out a name, you check it off." She began to erase names from the circles (which represented tables) and scribbled in new ones.

It was like a game, actually. We knew that Mona and Ariel couldn't sit together and that Mickey and his new wife couldn't sit with either of them, or with Zoey's mother. Zoey also tried to balance how many men and women sat at each table.

When it was done, Patrick stretched and yawned. "Wow, that was fun," he said.

Zoey gave him a Look.

Patrick strolled over to one side of the room. Picking up the television remote, he said, "I'm going to take myself out to the ball game. It's the Giants and the Braves. Would anyone care to join me in the box seats?" He motioned toward the sofa.

Sam jumped up eagerly. Charlie followed more slowly. I was about to join them when Zoey said, "And I'm about to try on my wedding dress. You want to help, Kristy?"

Well, no. I'd rather watch baseball. Zoey didn't

know me very well or she would never have asked the question.

I smiled politely. "Sure," I said.

As I followed Zoey out of the room, Sam caught my eye and made a goofy face. I stuck my tongue out at him.

It was a nice dress, simple and straight, with a high neck, tight sleeves, and a row of tiny pearly buttons down the back. The fabric was a pale ice-green.

I fished for the right word when Zoey turned to face me, and I came up with it. "Elegant," I said. "But it's not white . . ." I let my voice trail off.

Zoey laughed and looked pleased. "Thank you. No, it's not white. This is my first wedding, but after watching my father's fourth wife, Maude, trip down the aisle, dressed all in white ruffles and lace, I just couldn't do it. It looked ridiculous. I mean, Maude's not that much older than me, but . . ." Now her voice trailed off.

I grinned. "It's your wedding. And you'll look elegant."

"Thanks," Zoey said. "Do you think the hemline is right? Wait, let me put on the shoes that go with it."

Poor Zoey. She was asking the wrong person for

fashion advice, from the length of her hemline to stocking choice to jewelry. But I did my best, mostly agreeing with everything she said. As far as I could tell when we were finished, she hadn't changed her plans for her outfit one bit, but she thanked me profusely for my help anyway.

I laughed self-consciously. "You're welcome. But I'm not much of a fashion expert. I guess no one told you. I'm more into sports, that sort of thing."

Who would have told her? I wondered, even as I spoke. It's not something Patrick knew about me. In fact, he knew very little about me.

Zoey smiled. "Like your father."

"Hey, I hope I have better taste in tuxes," I joked.

Zoey was smoothing the dress into its bag before returning it to the closet. "I just hope our kids like sports," she said. "Patrick will be crushed if at least one of them isn't the sports fan he is."

She turned and saw my face. "Kristy?" she said.

My mind was racing. Kids? Zoey and Patrick were having kids? Somehow, that possibility had never entered my mind. I was totally unprepared.

"Kristy?" said Zoey again. "Are you all right?"

"Did you know the word 'fan' comes from 'fanatic'?" I said. "I'd say that's true of me and Sam and Charlie. Not David Michael, though. At least, not yet."

Zoey gave me an odd look.

Why would they have kids? My thoughts raced on. After all, Patrick hadn't exactly been a model father to the four children he already has — especially David Michael, whom he seemed to have forgotten.

Then my stunned amazement began to turn to anger. If he wanted to have a family, shouldn't he at least have tried working things out with us first? What were we, the experimental model?

Zoey said, "Well, I'm an Oakland fan myself. But I can cheer for the Giants when I have to. You want to go back out to the box seats?"

I nodded numbly.

"Kristy — your father and I . . . I hope this is okay with you. I mean, I want us to be a family. Just because Patrick and I want children of our own doesn't mean that he loves you any less."

I couldn't stop myself. "Of course not," I said. "How could he?"

It was a double-edged remark, and Zoey knew it. But before she could say anything, I more or less charged out of the room and back to the ball game. I took a chair a long way from Patrick and sat down. I watched the game without really seeing it.

All of a sudden, I agreed with Charlie. I wanted to leave. Right then.

I felt hurt and sick and angry and disappointed. In fact, I felt just the way I had felt when, as a little kid, I realized that my father had gone forever.

❈ Chapter 11

The next day, Friday, Zoey closed the restaurant for the day. She was up early, supervising arrangements for the rehearsal dinner that night. From there, she went with her friend Jessica to meet her mother and grandmother at the train station and take them back to Jessica's house in Mill Valley, by way of the scenic route. With Charlie driving one car and Patrick driving the other (I rode with Charlie, and Sam rode with Patrick), we went to the airport to pick up Mickey and Maude, and Mona. After a few tense moments, during which everyone smiled a lot and Mickey patted Patrick on the back half a dozen times, we parted ways gratefully. Charlie and I took Mona, who looked an awful lot like Maude, with frosted hair and long-lashed blue eyes. Mona had on lots of perfume. She was wearing a pink pantsuit with a blue scarf that matched her eyes.

Maude was wearing pink and yellow.

I didn't point out any of the similarities, though. I didn't think it would be very tactful.

Mona chatted about her flight, the weather, her "good friend" James, who couldn't make it to the wedding, and what a "sweet girl" Zoey was. She eyed the Casa Madrone critically for a moment when we arrived, then smiled and pronounced it delightful. "Don't worry about me," she said. "I can find my way to the rehearsal dinner. Right now, I'm going to have a beauty sleep and then a manicure."

"Nice to meet you," I said.

"You're sweet children," Mona declared, then disappeared into the hotel in a cloud of perfume.

The moment Mona was out of the car, Charlie said, "I can't believe it."

He wasn't talking about Mona. He was talking about the news I'd given him that morning, on the ride to the airport, about Zoey and Patrick's plan to have children.

"I know," I said.

We arrived home about the same time as Patrick and Sam — just as Zoey was leaving again. She looked harried, but the tense look left her face when Patrick swept her up in his arms and spun her around the deck in a crazy sort of waltz. They stopped at the far end of the deck, their heads close together, and talked intensely for a few minutes. The chemistry between them was so strong that I could almost feel it where I stood by the back door.

Charlie made a noise that sounded like "Humph" and walked into the house, but I stayed a moment longer. Patrick stepped back and danced a little jig, and Zoey laughed. I thought maybe this was one of the reasons she loved him. I could see Zoey was a serious sort of person. Maybe Patrick's surface approach to life, his desire to laugh rather than to take things hard, balanced her in some way.

But you can't laugh all the time, I thought. What then?

It made me feel old to think like that. I turned away and went into the house.

And once again, we were alone with our father.

This time, we hadn't planned a picnic. Charlie picked up the remote and began to flick through the channels. But no baseball game appeared.

"Not wrestling," I said. "Puh-lease."

Reluctantly, Charlie turned off the television. "If I were home now, I could be playing baseball."

"Relax," said Sam. "Your place on the team is a lock." He turned to Patrick. "Charlie's got an awesome reach. You should see him on first base."

"I'm impressed," said Patrick. And he sounded as if he meant it.

"And Kristy coaches a little-kids' softball team," Sam went on. "She plays too."

"Coaching? Not easy, especially little kids," Patrick said.

"How do you know?" Charlie asked. "You haven't had much experience around little kids. Have you?"

"Well, no," said Patrick, refusing to be pulled into an argument. "But sportswriters hear these things." He winked at me.

I didn't wink back. I looked down at my feet.

"Sportswriting must be fun," Sam said.

Sam was so eager, trying so hard. He was doing his best to — what? Butter up Patrick? Smooth things over? Avoid anything hard and unpleasant?

Suddenly, I saw how very similar Sam and Patrick were. It didn't make me like Sam very much just then, although I realized that was unfair.

Charlie said, "Yeah, sportswriting must be fun. More fun than a family."

Patrick's face froze, but to my amazement, he

didn't lose his temper. He went to the kitchen and said, "Anybody want a smoothie?"

"Me," said Sam.

"No, thanks," I said.

"No," said Charlie.

As Sam and Patrick made smoothies, Patrick tried again. "Let's rehearse for that rehearsal dinner," he said. "Surprise Zoey. Be super-prepared."

"You mean, get dressed up for it now?" asked Sam, looking unhappy.

"No," said Charlie again. He folded his arms and leaned back in his chair.

"Yeah, well, I guess it is a little early. . . . Hey, I have an idea. Why don't we play some catch, work up an appetite for tonight's feast. And it *will* be a feast, I promise you. I'm not cooking it, but I planned the menu myself."

"Great idea," said Sam. "Just like we used to."

"No," said Charlie, for the third time.

"Charlie . . ." Sam began.

"*No,*" said Charlie.

Sam knew not to push Charlie too hard, especially in his present mood. He turned to me.

"I don't know," I said uncomfortably. I wanted to do something, *anything*. But I didn't want to seem to take sides.

"I've got extra gloves, plenty for everybody," Patrick said. He was hustling down the hall. "In my closet in the study."

Charlie went to his room. I hesitated a moment longer. Then I gave in.

Patrick, Sam, and I headed out to the strip of grass on one side of the house.

At first, after every catch, Sam would make some goofy or encouraging comment. But then he seemed to relax a little and I found that I was relaxing too. It was good to be outside on a perfect day, sending the ball through the air, catching it with a solid, satisfying thump.

We tossed the ball around for awhile, sliding into an easy rhythm. Then Patrick lifted his leg and caught one of my pitches beneath it. He went into an exaggerated windup and then sent a soft, floating, silly pitch Sam's way.

Not to be outdone, Sam waved his glove around, shielding his eyes as if he'd lost a towering drive to center field in the sun. When he caught the ball, he fell to the ground in amazement.

I burst out laughing. Sam and Patrick did too. And then we were off, in a game of silly pitches. Sam did an elaborate windup of his own and faked my socks off, pretending to throw a pitch but not actually releasing the ball at all. I didn't even realize it until I had reached out with my glove.

That prompted Patrick to tell the story of a pitcher who had thrown about a dozen balls to his first baseman, trying to hold a fast runner close to the base so he couldn't steal. Each time, the runner stepped back on the bag and the first baseman threw the ball back to the pitcher — until the last time.

"The last time, he only pretended to throw the ball back to the pitcher. The runner didn't realize it. He stepped off the base and the first baseman tagged him out."

Both Sam and I agreed it was an excellent play, and I made a mental note of it, in case I ever had the chance to use it someday. We tossed the ball and the conversation around some more, and Patrick unrolled stories from his days as a sportswriter. I pitched in with stories of the Krushers, the team I coach.

I suddenly realized that it was sort of like old times, when Patrick had been part of the family. The only difference was that I was older now, and he and Sam didn't have to be so careful to toss me a ball I could catch. And, of course, Charlie wasn't there. I pushed the thought of Charlie out of my mind. By the time the afternoon was over, we were pitching as if the gap of more than six years had never existed.

Then it was time to start dressing for the rehearsal dinner.

Fortunately, we didn't have to get all decked out. I put on khakis and a nice shirt, made sure my hair was combed and there wasn't any weird stuff stuck between my teeth, and went downstairs. Zoey had already come and gone, Sam told me. "She's even faster than you are about getting ready," he said.

Another point in Zoey's favor, I thought, sitting down on one of the high stools at the counter and picking up part of the newspaper that Sam had spread out there.

Patrick was the next to appear. Like Sam, he was wearing pants, a shirt, and a sports jacket, only his pants were white instead of khaki, and the sports jacket was plaid instead of navy blue. I blinked at the intense tropical colors of the plaid.

"What do you think?" asked Patrick, hooking his thumbs under the lapels. "It's one of my favorite jackets. I call it my good-luck jacket."

"Really? Why?" I asked.

He didn't seem to notice that I hadn't given him my opinion. "Because I almost always got answers to questions when I was wearing it. Makes you stand out in a crowd of sportwriters."

"Another basic baseball strategy, right?" Sam grinned at Patrick, and Patrick grinned back.

"Right." Patrick glanced at his watch.

At that moment, Charlie joined us. He stopped when he saw Sam and Patrick, and his hand went to his neck, tugging off his tie. "At least I don't have to wear a noose tonight," he said.

Now, I've heard Charlie and Sam call neckties nooses — and worse — often.

But Patrick didn't know that. His face darkened. It was clear that he'd taken Charlie's innocent comment the wrong way.

"Noose?" he said in a dangerously quiet voice. Before Charlie could respond, Patrick continued. "I've had about enough of your negativity, your put-downs, your nasty tone. Can't you at least, for just a little while, behave like a good son?"

Charlie's eyes flashed. "Behave like a good son?" he repeated. "Why should I? It's not as if you ever behaved like a good father."

"Well, I didn't have the chance, did I?" Patrick said. "You didn't exactly try to stay in touch."

"*We* didn't? We were just kids, in case you've forgotten!" Charlie shouted. "Half the time we didn't even know where you were. You were the one who was supposed to be keeping up with us. It's basic, Patrick, even for fathers who walk out on their families."

"Hey," I said.

"You guys," Sam said.

They ignored us.

"I *had* to go!" Patrick shouted. "I didn't have a choice!"

"You're breaking my heart," Charlie's voice lowered into heavy sarcasm.

"You think your mother made it easy? If I had visited, how do you think she would have reacted?"

"You'll never know, will you? But I guess I shouldn't be surprised you'd try to blame Mom for what you did." I don't think I'd ever seen Charlie so angry, not Charlie the calm, Charlie the controlled.

"How dare you judge me? You immature, spoiled — " Patrick was shouting at the top of his lungs.

And I suddenly heard myself shouting, "Stop it! Stop it! You leave Charlie alone. How dare you call him spoiled? When he took care of all of us after you left? When he quit the baseball team so he could come home after school with us? How spoiled is that? Tell me!"

"I can take care of myself, Kristy," Charlie said.

It was such a big-brother response that I would

have laughed at any other time. But I didn't. I rushed on. "You left us. *You* left *us*. You never even said good-bye, or that you were sorry, or *anything*. You haven't even bothered to *talk* to David Michael. And don't you *dare* blame Mom."

"Why shouldn't he?" Charlie said. "It's the *mature* thing to do."

Patrick seemed to deflate before my eyes. He looked at me and blinked, as if he had seen something he hadn't expected. Then he closed his mouth around the words he'd been about to fling at Charlie. But I could see he was still tremendously angry.

In the silence, Sam said, "Okay, we've had the bench-clearing brawl — a rhubarb, isn't that what you call it?" He directed this question at Patrick, but Patrick didn't answer.

Still trying, Sam said, "So now we need to go to the dinner, okay, guys?"

Charlie said, spitting the words out one by one, "I'm not going to the dinner. Why should I go watch someone as nice as Zoey marry a family-ditching loser like our father?"

I wanted to die. I saw the muscles in Patrick's jaw tighten and the rage blaze in his eyes. But he only said, "Fine." Then he turned to me. "Coming, Kristy?"

But I couldn't abandon Charlie. Instinctively, I moved closer to my oldest brother.

Patrick gave me a long look. I met his gaze steadily. Then he shrugged, as if it were no big deal. "Sam," said Patrick, turning aside and seeming to dismiss Charlie and me from his thoughts, his life.

Sam made an apologetic gesture. "I guess I'll, uh, stay here."

Patrick wheeled, picked up the car keys, and walked out of the house to go to the rehearsal dinner.

Alone.

❋ Chapter 12

"Go on if you want to. You can still catch him," Charlie said into the huge, roaring silence Patrick had left behind.

I sat back down on the stool at the counter. "No," I said dully.

Sam pulled a stool up next to me, propped his elbows on the counter, and dropped his forehead onto the heels of his hands. He kept his face down and I wondered for a moment if he was trying not to cry.

Charlie glanced at me. Then he sat down abruptly on the arm of the sofa. "I can fight my own battles, Kristy. But thanks."

"Yeah, well," I said. "I had something to say too."

"He deserved it," Charlie said. "And more."

Sam raised his head. "Good work, Chuck," he said with awful sarcasm.

"What's wrong with you? I said you could go without me," Charlie shot back.

"Like I'm going to leave you guys here," Sam said. "You're my family. Not Dad. Not like that."

I put my hand on Sam's shoulder.

"But he *is* our father," Sam went on. "Don't you get it? He's not perfect . . . "

"Duh," said Charlie.

"Shut up! Shut up and let me finish," Sam said. "He's not perfect, he's not even close to perfect. But he's our father!"

Charlie and I looked at Sam. I could feel his shoulder shaking beneath my hand. Unnerved, I removed it.

"You think I'm some kind of wimp because I want to get along with Dad? Because I want to forgive him and put it behind me? Well, I'm not. I was there too when he left, remember? You think I didn't miss him? You think I didn't wonder why he left?"

"Sam," said Charlie.

"You think I didn't hate him? That I didn't wonder whether maybe, if I'd been a better kid, he wouldn't have left?"

"Sam!" I cried out, shocked.

"But I grew up anyway, Charlie. And I decided to come to the wedding. I decided to make the best of it. And I'm sick of you pouting like a — a — a six-year-old."

I looked at Sam. I said softly, "I thought it was my fault. That he left. And you know what? I thought if I was really good, he might come back."

Charlie thumped his fist on the arm of the sofa. "That's not true. That's not why he left. He left because he's irresponsible. We were keeping him from his big career as a sportswriter. Some big career *that* turned out to be."

"But we were just kids. We didn't understand," Sam said softly. "Any more than you did, Charlie."

Charlie didn't say anything for a long moment. Then he said, looking out the window, "Patrick used to spend hours practicing pitching and grounding with me. We'd get up early to do it, before even you were awake, Sam."

"I know. I'd wake up and you'd be dressed and gone. I remember Mom calling you guys in for breakfast, even in bad weather."

"And you guys taught me to play," I said. "Remember? We'd have games on Saturdays? Patrick would organize us into teams — everyone who wanted to play. All the kids in the neighborhood could join in." I paused and said, "Who knows? Maybe that's where I got the idea for the Krushers."

"You remember that time Mom and Dad took us all to see the women's state playoffs?" Sam said. "That was so much fun. Dad knew everybody. And he had these great seats because he was a sports-writer."

I had a sudden flash of memory: a crowd, Mom and Dad laughing, the smell of hot dogs and pop-corn.

"I remember," I said.

"He really likes sports," said Charlie.

"We all do," I said.

Sam nodded, then smiled a little and said, "But I don't ever remember him liking to cook."

"Yeah. Who would ever believe he'd trade in a baseball glove for an oven mitt?" Charlie said.

"You think he talks about baseball in the kitchen? Or sports?" Sam said.

"I bet he tells stories all the time," I said.

Sam held up his hand. "Now, this steak," he said in a deep voice, motioning to an imaginary piece of meat in his hand. "It reminds me of that old baseball saying about this pitcher, you ever heard it? 'He could throw a lamb chop past a wolf.' "

We all laughed, and I felt the tension in my body ease.

"I guess he's changed. Some," I said.

"And I guess he's stayed the same. A lot," said Charlie.

"We get the point, Charlie," Sam said. "But get this point: Patrick's not ever going to live up to our expectations of him, not the ones we had when we were children. And we're not kids anymore."

"So I should lower my expectations," Charlie said. He made a face. "Great."

"Is that so bad?" Sam ask. "To lower the expectations you had when you were a kid?"

"I guess I don't expect Santa Claus to come down the chimney anymore," I said.

"Or maybe I shouldn't have any expectations at all," Charlie said, and I could tell he didn't like the idea. Something in me twisted and I realized I didn't like it either.

Sam looked down at his feet. "Maybe," he said softly.

I think it was at that moment I gave up, finally and forever, the idea of Patrick as my dad.

I said, trying to keep my voice from cracking, "After all, we've got a great family. Without Patrick."

Without Patrick.

"I guess he's trying," Charlie said. "But don't forget, I didn't want to come to this wedding in the first place. I only did it because you guys practically begged me."

"Well, you're here now," Sam said. "And Patrick is what he is. He's trying, at least. Why can't you try too, just for this one week? It's a lot better, a lot easier, than hating him."

"But I don't hate him," Charlie said. He paused. "I don't hate him," he repeated.

I jumped up. "Hey, what's the point of getting all dressed up with no place to go?" I said. "Let's go to the rehearsal dinner."

I held my breath. But Sam was on his feet immediately. "We should. For Zoey if not for Dad."

We both looked at Charlie. "Well?" Sam said. "Do we call a cab or what?"

"Start dialing," said Charlie, standing up too. "I guess . . . I guess we can't strand him on third base. He doesn't deserve a great team like us. But somebody's got to be on his side."

✿ Chapter 13

The rehearsal dinner was just ending when we arrived. The crowd wasn't a big one, and we made quite an entrance.

Patrick stared at us.

Zoey was the first to her feet. "Oh, good," she said. "I'm so glad you could make it." She held out her hands to us as she hurried forward.

"I'm hungry," Sam blurted out. "It smells great."

"I think we can still give you a little something to eat," Zoey said. "Who haven't you met?"

Patrick was on his feet now too. The smile he gave us was uncertain.

Charlie stepped forward and held out his hand. "Sorry we're late," he said.

Patrick took Charlie's hand and shook it vigorously. "That's okay," he said. "You made it."

He shook hands with Sam and then he hugged me so hard it made me gasp.

Zoey introduced us to everyone, even the waiters. As they poured more coffee, she somehow managed to clear away three places at the table where she'd been sitting with Patrick.

"Stay here," she said to Patrick. "I'll start organizing people to go over to the veranda."

We ate hastily as Zoey moved from one table to the other. "She looks like a sheepherder," I observed.

Patrick, who'd been uncharacteristically silent, suddenly laughed. "True. And keep in mind that a few of those are wolves in sheep's clothing. This is the first time that some of these people have been in the same room together for years. . . . It reminds me of the time I was at this sports awards dinner. The finalists were two guys who absolutely hated each other. No one knew what to expect. They were at opposite ends of the guests of honor table, but you could feel the tension. And you know how it is with writing. You can't help hoping, maybe a little, that something wild and crazy will happen, just to make an ordinary story interesting."

Patrick, cheerful and possibly a little hyper from relief, rattled on as Zoey rejoined us and we quickly ate our dinner. Then we hurried to the veranda on the hill, where the wedding was to be held.

It had an amazing view, especially with the sun going down. I stopped for a moment to stare out over the water, trying to get my bearings. If I was facing west, what was on the other side? And which way was home?

Charlie said, "I have to tell you, Zoey, I'm not going to be in the wedding."

She only nodded, then motioned to Patrick. He took the news calmly enough. "If that's the way you feel, then," he said.

"Sam's going to be in it. You'll have a best man," Charlie said.

"No," said Sam, making a joke as always. "*The* best man."

Then the rehearsal began — and stopped almost immediately.

"No!" cried Maude, Mr. Amberson's fourth wife, pressing both hands to her chest dramatically. She reminded me for a moment of my stepsister, Karen, who is also fond of melodrama. "Oh, *no!*"

Zoey, who had been about to proceed down the aisle (made up of a single row of chairs on either side, in which we were all sitting) stopped obediently.

I saw the look of anticipation and amusement on

Patrick's face and guessed that he was hoping, well, for the worst.

"What is it, Maude?" Zoey asked. "Are you okay?"

Maude rushed forward and tugged at Zoey's arm. "It's *terrible* luck for the bride to participate in the rehearsal. You can't do it. You must have someone stand in for you."

"She's right," said Mona.

"It's true," agreed Ariel. Then the two ex-wives and the current wife looked at one another, startled. I don't think they'd ever expected to agree on anything.

The moment of harmony vanished, though, when Mona said, "I'll stand in for you, Zoey."

"No, I will," said Ariel.

"Don't be silly," said Maude. "I'm the one who thought of it. I can do it, Zoey, dear."

"I don't believe this," Zoey's father said, his bushy gray eyebrows snapping together in a frown. "You already got married once this year, Maude. Isn't that enough for you?"

Zoey's mother made a sound that might have been laughter and Zoey's grandmother said to her, in what she must have imagined was a low voice, "Not if it was to *him*."

The look of unholy glee on Patrick's face grew. He stepped back two paces and waited to see what would happen. Zoey looked around desperately. Her father hadn't heard what his former mother-in-law had said, but almost everyone else had.

"Why don't I do it?" I heard myself volunteer. "It'd be fun."

Now I heard a smothered snort from where Sam was standing by the altar. He knew, and Charlie did too, that standing up in a wedding rehearsal was *not* my idea of a good time.

"Thank you, Kristy. Why don't we let Kristy join in the fun?" Zoey said.

What could anyone say? Everyone nodded and smiled and said what a fine idea it was, then resumed their battle stations on either side of the aisle.

Stepping aside, Zoey rolled her eyes at me. I took her place, and we went through the rehearsal. Sam escorted Zoey's best friend, Jessica, who was her maid of honor, down the aisle, and they parted at the table that was serving as the stand-in for the altar. I followed alone.

Since the wedding wasn't going to be a big one, the rehearsal didn't take long. We walked through it once, then took a quick break while Zoey and the minister consulted on something. I found myself standing by Zoey's mom, Jeannie Amberson. Mrs. Argos, Zoey's grandmother, and Ariel had begun an animated conversation, at least animated on Zoey's grandmother's part. She was telling Ariel all about her own wedding.

"Well done, Kristy," said Ms. Amberson. "You stepped in and saved what could have been a bit of a messy situation."

"No problem," I said.

"I'm glad you and your brothers could make it out for the wedding. I know that's one of the reasons Zoey wanted to have it in the summer, so it wouldn't interfere with school."

"Oh," I said. "That was nice of her." I didn't know what else to say.

"You know," Ms. Amberson went on, "I'm surprised that Zoey is getting married. She was always so independent. I hope Patrick can understand that and appreciate it."

"I think he will," I said. I watched as Patrick slipped his arm around Zoey and whispered in her ear. She nodded, smiling up at him, and his whole face was changed by the simple, happy smile he gave back to her. "It's pretty obvious he loves her."

The minister raised her hands and said, "Once more, just to be sure, everyone."

We went back to our positions. Patrick and Charlie were talking quietly at one side of the altar. Had Charlie changed his mind about being a best man?

But no. I saw Charlie shake his head. Patrick gave Charlie a nod and an awkward pat on the shoulder and Charlie returned to his seat.

We returned home in comfortable silence. I discovered, as I walked into the house, that I was tired, and I said so.

"Me too," said Charlie. "See you guys in the morning." He made a quick exit. Sam and I hung around long enough to check the late-night box scores for baseball, then retreated to our rooms.

A little while later, as I turned back the covers of one of the twin beds in the room, a tap sounded on the door.

"Come in," I said.

Zoey opened the door. "I have a favor to ask," she said. "Can I sleep in here tonight?"

My heart jumped. Had she and Patrick had a fight?

Seeing the alarm in my face, Zoey laughed.

"Don't worry. It's just another one of those wedding customs. The groom isn't supposed to see the bride on the morning of the wedding. I put all my stuff in the study, and I'm going to get dressed there. Mom and Grandmama and Jessica are coming over to help."

"Sure," I said.

"Thanks," said Zoey.

She settled into the other bed, reached out, and turned off the bedside light. About half a second later, she turned it on again.

"I can't sleep," she announced. "At least, not right away. Would it bother you if I read or something? Or I could go downstairs. Maybe make some hot chocolate, except I don't really want any — unless you do? Maybe I could fix you some?"

She'd swung her feet over the side of the bed and I registered the fact that the oversize nightshirt she was wearing was printed with coffee cups.

"No, thanks," I said.

Zoey settled back. She reached out to turn off the light.

Somehow, I wasn't surprised when, maybe ninety seconds later, she turned it on again.

"Kristy," she said. "Are you sleepy?"

I had to laugh. And laughing woke me up a little. "Not really," I said half truthfully.

"I'm not sleepy at all. I should be exhausted. I must be nervous about tomorrow. How could I be? I mean, we practiced this already. This is just the dress-up version, right? Nothing to be nervous about. The rehearsal wasn't perfect, but hey, break a leg, right?"

"Uh, right," I said. "Bad rehearsal, good show. If the rehearsal had gone well, then you'd have something to worry about."

I liked Zoey more than ever at that moment. I sat up, fluffed my pillow, and turned to look at her.

"I keep thinking there's something I've forgotten," Zoey said.

"Something old, something new, something borrowed, something blue?" I asked.

"Done, done, done, and done."

We were silent for a moment. Then I said, "Zoey, I . . . "

At the exact same instant, Zoey began, "Kristy, there's . . . "

We stopped. We stared at each other. Zoey said, "You first."

I hadn't known I was going to say it, but suddenly, there I was, blurting it out. "Zoey, I don't know what Patrick has told you. But in case you wondered why Charlie's been a little bit hostile, it's because Patrick . . . hasn't been a great father. In fact, he's been the father who wasn't there, especially for David Michael."

Zoey drew her knees up and clasped her hands around them. I continued. "He just walked out on us. I guess he had reasons a little kid couldn't understand, but that's the way it seemed to me, at least. And to Charlie and Sam. I've heard from him the most, but that's just a couple of postcards and birthday cards and some random meetings."

"I know," Zoey said softly.

"And you talked about having a family. Well, what if he does the same thing to you that he did to us? I mean, I can't tell if he's changed. How could I? I was just six when he left."

"I know," Zoey said again.

"He told you everything?" I was surprised. Telling the unpleasant truth didn't strike me as one of my father's strong points, then or now. He preferred to go away, avoid trouble — unless, of course, it didn't involve him and would make a good story.

Shaking her head, Zoey said, "Some. Not much. Not in so many words. I made him tell me a good bit of it. He talked about you a lot, but it didn't take a rocket scientist to realize that the stories he told all stopped when you were six and Charlie was just ten and Sam was, what, eight or nine? And all your photographs were the same — pictures of little kids. And a baby."

"You made him tell you?" I couldn't imagine anyone making my father do anything. And yet, Zoey had already proved herself able to exercise the power of persuasion on my dad, at least with regard to tuxedos.

"I did," said Zoey. "He didn't like it. But he didn't like the alternative either."

"Oh," I said.

"I think your mother must be a brave woman," Zoey said out of the blue. "To raise such great kids on her own. And I think it's too bad that their father was a charming little boy who couldn't handle the responsibility."

Whoa. Zoey wasn't holding back.

"But Kristy, it's been a lot of years. Your father's grown up." She smiled. "At least, somewhat. I suspect he'll always be one of those guys who's a bit of a kid. He'll be an especially great father when our kids are young."

"And then what?" I couldn't help asking.

"And then, I believe, he'll stay to watch them

grow up. How could he not, after realizing what he missed with you guys? He's finally learned, I think, that the grass isn't always greener on the other side of the fence."

"Maybe," I said.

"Listen, I want you to know that I love Patrick, and he loves me. And he wants to love you, and to see more of you in the future, if you'll let him. If you'll let us."

"I guess we could work something out," I answered.

Suddenly, Zoey yawned, then sneezed, then fell back on her pillow. "I'm sleepy," she said in amazement.

Yawns are contagious. I said, around a yawn of my own, "Me too."

Zoey turned off the light a third time. In the darkness she said, "Don't worry, Kristy. It'll be okay. And thanks for listening."

"Thanks for talking," I replied, and meant it.

Zoey rolled over and, I think, fell asleep almost immediately.

But I stayed awake to worry a little while longer. Zoey, I concluded, was much cooler than my father. Like my brothers, I wasn't sure exactly what she saw in him, but she didn't seem to be blind and smitten. She wasn't just a kid marrying her first love. So maybe it would be okay.

I hoped so, for Zoey's sake as much as for my father's, and perhaps just a little bit more.

❋ Chapter 14

"What a great day for a wedding," sang Patrick, throwing his arms out wide. "What do you think, Kristy? I ordered it up special."

I smiled and walked out onto the deck. "You did an excellent job."

"How'd Zoey sleep? You girls stay up all night talking about weddings?"

"Something like that."

He put his arm around my shoulders and gave me a hug. "And she still wants to go through with it?" he teased.

Not quite sure how to take that, I said, "Zoey's very strong-minded."

My father gave a shout of laughter. "You mean stubborn," he said. "And a good thing too. I have to tell you, I didn't sleep a wink. So I woke up Sam and we watched Australian football reruns. Have you ever watched Australian football?"

I shook my head. "Not really."

"We should have watched the celebrity wrestling," Patrick said sorrowfully.

Now it was my turn to laugh. My father, I thought, probably *could* charm the birds out of the trees.

"What's so funny?" Sam said, shuffling onto the deck to join us, one hand wrapped around a glass of orange juice.

"You are," I said. "Your hair is sticking straight up."

Sam yawned hugely and slurped some juice.

"Anybody else thirsty?" Patrick asked. "Kristy?"

"No, thanks," I said, and Patrick disappeared inside.

I looked at Sam. "How's it going?"

"He's nervous," said Sam. "Like a little kid. Excited."

"Like a little kid," I echoed, and remembered what Zoey had said about Patrick-the-kid the night before.

I had wandered back out onto the deck later when a car pulled into the driveway. I recognized Jessica. She had brought Mrs. Argos and Ms.

Amberson. It was time for the bride to start getting dressed.

The back door banged open. "Kristy," said Patrick, "why don't you make some coffee for everyone? Come on, Sam my man. It's time we got dressed."

"But — " I began to protest.

It was too late. Patrick had made his escape, banging the door again. Sam gave me a grin and vanished too, just like the Cheshire Cat on a bad-hair day.

After that, things picked up speed. I have only a blurred memory of the events leading up to the wedding. I made coffee while Jessica and Zoey's mother and grandmother joined Zoey. I put a thermal carafe of it on a tray, along with some mugs, sugar, and milk. Jessica swooped down on it gratefully and so did Ms. Amberson. But when Zoey reached for a mug, her mother said, "No! Don't drink that."

"Why? Is it bad luck?" asked Zoey, but she lowered the mug obediently.

"Nerves," said Ms. Amberson. She looked at me. "Is there anything without caffeine?"

Zoey rolled her eyes but she handed the mug of coffee back to me. "We have herbal tea in the cupboard next to the sink," she said.

"I'll make some," I said.

As it turned out, Zoey didn't drink the herbal tea either. By the time I returned with it, she was wrestling with her stockings and muttering under her breath.

She went from muttering to threats of stocking-murder when she ran the first two pairs. Jessica and Mrs. Argos both produced extra pairs and looked sheepishly at each other as Zoey burst out laughing. "I guess I don't have to worry about people not being prepared." She sobered and added, "Except maybe me. What time is it?"

"You have plenty of time," Jessica said. "And I even have more stockings. Take it easy."

But Zoey was beginning to feel nervous, I could tell. I slipped out to get ready myself.

When I peeked in Zoey's room again, she was sitting on the floor in her wedding dress, her eyes closed and her head tilted back.

"What happened?" I gasped. "Did she faint?"

Jessica said, "Relaxation technique. Deep breathing."

"I just wish she wouldn't do it on the floor in her wedding dress," Ms. Amberson said.

"What time is it?" Zoey asked, letting out air like a teakettle letting off steam.

"You have plenty of time," her mother said.

"You do," I agreed. "And anyway, they can't start without you."

"Right," said Zoey. She inhaled, and I closed the door and went out to the living room.

Zoey's grandmother, Mrs. Argos, was there. She was sitting in what I thought of as Patrick's chair, a recliner lined up in front of the television, only she had turned it to face the windows. She had raised the footrest and taken her shoes off.

"Relaxation technique," she said with a smile when she saw me.

I burst out laughing.

"Come," Mrs. Argos said, grinning more broadly. "Sit. It's going to be a long day."

I sat. I took my shoes off. I propped up my feet on the coffee table.

Patrick and Sam emerged. "Is the coast clear?" Patrick asked in a stage whisper.

"All clear," I whispered back.

He and Sam walked out, looking self-consciously pleased with themselves. They looked splendid. I jumped up to get Patrick's camera. "Don't move."

I took a photo of Sam and Patrick. Then Charlie came downstairs. He agreed, after only a slight hesitation, to be photographed with Sam and Patrick.

Then Mrs. Argos took a photo of me with Sam, Charlie, and our father (I didn't realize until I saw the print that I had forgotten to put my shoes back on).

We heard a door open.

"Go," commanded Zoey's mother. "Shoo. The bridegroom can't see the bride until she is walking down the aisle."

Sam and Patrick ran like rabbits out of the house. I had to laugh.

My laughter turned to a gasp of admiration when I saw Zoey. She was beautiful.

"Zoey!" said her grandmother. She beamed. "Always the smartest and the prettiest. Still it's true."

"Oh, Grandmama," Zoey said, and threw her arms around her grandmother.

We made it to the wedding on time.

Charlie and I sat with Zoey's mother and grandmother. Zoey's dad and Maude sat across the aisle. Mona sat across the aisle from Ariel, who sat behind Charlie, leaning forward to whisper to him whenever she felt like it. The music began, a crash of triumphant sound that *wasn't* the traditional wedding march. I jumped a little.

Patrick and Sam joined the minister, a short

woman in clerical robes. Everyone turned as Jessica walked down the aisle, followed by Zoey.

Even though I had seen her just a little while before, I blinked in amazement at the transformation. As she walked steadily up the aisle, her eyes were locked on Patrick. I had a feeling she didn't know the rest of us were there at all, at least not at that moment.

Patrick stepped forward and took her hand, and his smile lit up his face.

Had he and my mom looked at each other that way at their wedding?

What had happened?

I wondered if I would ever know.

Then the minister began to speak, and I focused on the service.

It was short, and Ms. Amberson, Maude, Mona, and Ariel all cried. Zoey's grandmother didn't. Both Mr. Amberson and Ms. Amberson stood up when the minister asked who was giving the bride in marriage.

Then she said, "I now pronounce you husband and wife. You may kiss the bride," and it was over.

They walked down the aisle to "Take Me Out to the Ball Game."

After that, there was a great party. We headed for

the Greenhouse, which looked like a fairy tale come to life. We ate and talked and Sam made a funny toast.

Then, just when I thought the toasts were over, Charlie stood up. He cleared his throat and I felt my body grow tense. I clutched the edge of the chair under the table.

"I just want to say to Patrick and Zoey, best wishes. I hope you have a wonderful life together." He sat down abruptly.

Patrick stood up and looked at Charlie for a long moment. Then he smiled and said softly, "Thank you, Charlie." And then he looked out at us and said, "Thank you all. Now, let's dance!"

The band began to play. Patrick and Zoey stepped onto the dance floor and swept around the room. After that, Zoey danced with her father.

And Patrick walked across the room and bowed — to me.

I stood up, not sure what to do. Charlie said, firmly but kindly, "Go on."

Patrick offered me his arm and led me out onto the dance floor.

"It was a beautiful wedding," I said.

"One of the things that made it so beautiful was your being here," said Patrick. "Thank you, Kristy."

I felt a lump in my throat. "Sure," I replied.

I saw Charlie leading Ms. Amberson onto the dance floor, and then I saw Sam leaning over and offering his hand to Zoey's grandmother. And then we were all dancing and I was suddenly so happy, that, well . . .

I could have danced all night.

❀ Chapter 15

"So that's how it went," I concluded.

Mom and I were sitting in Adirondack chairs in the shady backyard, drinking lemonade, talking a little, being quiet a little. We had the whole place to ourselves. Charlie and Sam had taken Emily Michelle, David Michael, and Andrew to the park. Karen was with her two best friends at a pool party. Nannie and Watson had gone to the public library's annual fund-raiser — a plant sale.

I'd been telling Mom about the wedding in between stretches of comfortable, it's-good-to-be-home silence. Only I didn't think of it as the wedding, I thought of it as The Wedding. Of all the weddings I'd been a part of, this was the one that would stand out for me for a long, long time.

"I wish Patrick well," Mom said. "And Zoey."

I glanced at my mom. I could tell she meant it. Whatever bad feelings Mom had had about Patrick were gone. She certainly didn't love him anymore, I realized, but she wasn't angry anymore either.

It occurred to me then that Mom was very happy. That she loved her life. I looked down at the lemonade and laughed.

"What?" Mom asked.

"Life gave our family some lemons and we made lemonade," I said. I wasn't calling Patrick a lemon, not exactly. But Mom knew what I meant. She smiled. I went on. "I hope Patrick sticks around and doesn't disappear this time, just because of a few lemons."

Raising her glass in a toast, Mom said, "Here's to lemonade made with your own lemons. It's the sweetest and the best."

I heard a car turn into the driveway and recognized the rattling thump of Charlie's engine. Doors slammed. Charlie said, "Don't slam the door."

"I didn't," I heard David Michael say.

"Will it fall off?" Andrew said.

"Hey, Charlie, what has four doors and is yellow?" I heard Sam say.

"A lemon," Charlie said. "That joke is *so* old."

"I don't get it," David Michael said.

Their voices were growing muffled as they headed toward the house. I heard Emily Michelle laugh and say, "Jemonnnn."

"Because a crummy car is called a lemon, see?" Sam said.

"No," said David Michael.

I looked at Mom. We started to laugh.

"You really do look good in a dress," Claudia said, leaning over to study the photographs critically. Zoey the efficient (no wonder I liked her — she reminded me of me) had had some of the candid wedding photos developed at a one-hour place and had given Charlie, Sam, and me a set just before we'd boarded the plane. The official wedding photographs would come later.

"Very good," agreed Stacey. "You should wear a dress."

"No," I interrupted. "Forget it. It's a nice dress. But even a nice dress could never be as comfortable as jeans."

"True," said Claudia, who was herself wearing cutoff jeans over bicycle shorts, and suspenders she'd decorated with buttons. Beneath that, she was wearing a paint-splattered T-shirt, which she called her tribute to Jackson Pollock.

Jackson Pollock is, I think, a painter.

I was in cutoffs and a Cynthia Cooper WNBA shirt.

Cynthia Cooper is an MVP basketball player.

Mary Anne was in khaki shorts and a faded polo shirt. Stacey had opted for linen overall shorts and a ribbed sleeveless undershirt the exact color of her eyes.

We were in Claudia's room. We had just finished our BSC meeting. Things had gone smoothly while I was away, so there wasn't a whole lot to catch up on. We took a few calls and tried to plan ahead for the back-to-school rush. Now we were preparing to order pizza and do some serious hanging out for the rest of the evening. I was in wedding recovery mode.

Picking up another photograph, Mary Anne squinted at it. "Patrick?" she said.

"Got it in one," I replied.

"He looks good," said Mary Anne. "He doesn't look different at all from when we were little."

I looked at my father and realized that it was true. The Patrick who smiled out at us from this new photograph was the exact same Patrick (except for shorter hair) who smiled in all the old photographs we still had in the album in the attic.

"No, he hasn't changed," I said. "It's weird.

Mom looks different. I look different. Charlie and Sam look different, and, of course, David Michael isn't a baby anymore. But Patrick is exactly the same."

"Like Peter Pan," said Claudia. "You know. He never grows up. He never grows old."

"And he lives in never-never land," said Stacey. "Peter Pan, I mean. Not Patrick."

"But Patrick does too," I said slowly. "I don't mean California. I mean in a world where, if something doesn't work out right away, he gets mad. Or he quits. Or leaves."

"Like a little kid playing with toys," Mary Anne said.

"Yeah."

"Poor Patrick," said Mary Anne.

I looked at her in surprise.

"Well, think about it. We've been friends forever, practically. We've had fights and we've disagreed and we've apologized and we've, we've . . . "

"Gone to art shows, even though some of us don't like art," Claudia said, taking up the theme.

"We always like *your* art," I assured her, and she grinned.

Stacey said, "And we've been here for one another when our parents left or got divorced or remarried. When I had problems with diabetes, you guys helped me pull it together."

"And all those baby-sitting disasters," I said, seeing in my mind's eye the baseballs going through windows and bathtubs overflowing and kids running away and hiding and a hundred other moments in our careers.

"And successes," Mary Anne pointed out. "See what I mean? Patrick didn't stick around for things like that. He doesn't have the same memories. Or friends. How can he, when he didn't hang in there for them the way we have for one another?"

We were silent for a moment. Finally, I said, "He doesn't have the family he could have had either. It could have been a different wedding if Patrick had only tried to stay in touch with us, tried to be a part of our lives, instead of ducking out."

"Right," agreed Claudia.

I said, "I still don't know how I feel about him. I mean, I love him, because he's my father. But I don't know if I'll ever like him very much."

It was weird, saying that about my own father. It kind of hurt, deep in my chest. But I felt a sense of relief, saying it out loud.

No one seemed surprised or horrified. Even softhearted Mary Anne nodded. She patted my arm.

I took a deep breath. "He could change," I said.

"Maybe he will," Claudia said diplomatically.

"And if he doesn't, well, I'm still . . . pretty lucky," I concluded. I was getting sentimental. I could tell, because Mary Anne's eyes looked suspiciously shiny, as if she were blinking back tears.

"You are," agreed Stacey. "You've got a cool family — and the coolest friends in the entire world."

"You're right," I said. "And I just want you guys to know that if you decide to get married someday, I'll wear a dress to your weddings."

"You have to," said Mary Anne seriously. "If you're going to be a bridesmaid."

"You don't *have* to wear dresses in weddings," Stacey observed. "People have all kinds of weddings."

"I'm going to design all the clothes that people wear in my wedding, if I get married," Claudia said. Her eyes took on a faraway look. "It'll be like an art installation. Wow. This is a great idea for an art piece. I could . . . "

"Good grief," I said. "Let's order some pizza."

And so we did.

About the Author

ANN MATTHEWS MARTIN was born on August 12, 1955. She grew up in Princeton, NJ, with her parents and her younger sister, Jane.

Although Ann used to be a teacher and then an editor of children's books, she's now a full-time writer. She gets ideas for her books from many different places. Some are based on personal experiences. Others are based on childhood memories and feelings. Many are written about contemporary problems or events.

All of Ann's characters, even the members of the Baby-sitters Club, are made up. (So is Stoneybrook.) But many of her characters are based on real people. Sometimes Ann names her characters after people she knows; other times she chooses names she likes.

In addition to the Baby-sitters Club books, Ann Martin has written many other books for children. Her favorite is *Ten Kids, No Pets* because she loves big families and she loves animals. Her favorite BSC book is *Kristy's Big Day.* (Kristy is her favorite baby-sitter.)

Ann M. Martin now lives in New York with her cats, Gussie, Woody, and Willy, and her dog, Sadie. Her hobbies are reading, sewing, and needlework — especially making clothes for children.

Friends *Baby-sitters Club* Forever

Look for #2

STACEY VS. CLAUDIA

"I hate to tell you this, Stacey," Kristy said, "but she's more than a little mad. What happened?"

I sighed. There was no sense trying to hide this. Kristy and Mary Anne were bound to find out. "It's about Jeremy," I replied, sitting on Claudia's bed. "It turns out that he likes — "

Claudia returned, holding a paper plate of carrots, some dip splashed messily on top of them. "Here," she said, thrusting the plate at me.

The carrots flew onto my lap, dip smearing my clothes. I jumped up. "You did that on purpose!" I accused her.

"I did not. Look what you did to my bed! It's got dip all over it."

"It's not my fault you threw food at me!"

"Oh, no, nothing's your fault. I forgot that.

You're never to blame. You can do whatever you like and it doesn't matter."

"It's just dip," Kristy said. "It'll wash out."

Claudia just glared at me as she left the room. She returned with a wet towel and began wiping her bed.

I picked up a carrot stick that hadn't hit the floor and bit into it.

"Okay," Kristy said. "Here's some club business I'd like to discuss. Since there're only four of us now I think we have to coordinate our weekend activities. We can't *all* be unavailable on the weekends at the same time or our clients will stop calling entirely."

"But what can we do?" Mary Anne asked. "Logan's already annoyed that I'm not always available on the weekends. Since we're down to four members it's really been hard."

"Maybe we should assign free-time slots," Kristy suggested. "We could rotate them from week to week and — "

"Stacey can't do that," Claudia cut in. "She'll be needing all her free time since she's stealing everyone's boyfriends."

"That is a lie!" I cried, outraged.

"*What* is going on?" Kristy demanded.

"She's trying to take Jeremy from me!" Claudia cried.

"I'm not! You don't have him anyway!"

"This is bad," Mary Anne muttered, looking as if she wished she were somewhere else.

"Can we talk about this later?" Kristy asked. "Right now I'd like to talk about a rotating weekend schedule."

"Who cares about that when everything in my life is falling apart?" Claudia said.

"Oh, come on," I said. "Your life isn't falling apart."

"It isn't? The boy I'm crazy about couldn't care less about me, and my best friend turns out to be a two-timing back stabber!"

"Are you both really that crazy about Jeremy?" Mary Anne asked.

"Yes!" we answered together.

We looked at each other fiercely.

"Stacey, I don't want you anywhere near Jeremy," said Claudia.

"Guess what, Claudia," I came back at her. "After the things you've said — I don't really care what you want anymore."